HELLCAT BOOK 3

NEW EDEN

WILLIAM VITKA

A PERMUTED PRESS BOOK
ISBN: 978-1-68261-249-1
ISBN (eBook): 978-1-68261-250-7

New Eden
Hellcat Book Three
© 2016 by William Vitka
All Rights Reserved

Cover art by Christian Bentulan

PERMUTED
PRESS

Permuted Press, LLC
permutedpress.com

Published in the United States of America

Also by William Vitka

The Hroza Connection series
Stranded
Emergence
Live, from the End of the World
A Man and His Robot
Blood God
Kill Machine

Bartender series
Bartender
Hitman
Godless

Hellcat series
Nightmare Highway
Blood on the Tracks
New Eden

1.

The Hellcat roars in the morning light. Up in these goddamn mountains. The hills. Bullet holes in the rear bumper make an incessant whistle are air passes over em.

The Rockies loom ahead. Caps in the distance stark white against the sky. Snow and icy particulates sail and swirl along the rapid winds.

Athena keeps her eyes on the road ahead. Interstate 70. Curves in the blacktop. Tunnels that cut through the stone.

She's got no words for Michelle. Seems like the pregnant woman ain't got any words for her, either. So silence hangs between em.

With Athena's mp3 player gone since Frankie's—and no signal on the radio to hear Dapper Dan and Don outta Columbus—the only sound inside is the V8 of the Hellcat. The monster under the hood. And, every once in a while, the flick of Athena's lighter.

The interstate here is the same as everywhere else: littered with a few useless wrecks, but otherwise cleared of anything that could be scavenged.

Question here ain't so much who did the scavenging— probably the Rangers in Denver—but as always, who the fuck's gonna get in Athena's way now.

Hopefully, nobody.

Athena thinks: *Wish in one hand, shit in the other.*

Another issue that ain't been dealt with at all? Michelle's end game. The idea that the Hellcat driver's supposed to ferry the pregnant broad out to some safe haven for her soon-to-pop baby.

That damned baby.

Athena's goal remains the same.

She wants to die her own way. Go to sleep in the redwoods while the sun sets.

Never wake up again.

Course, Michelle's inconsequential to that.

But...She's also become a strange fixture in Athena's life. This young, almost comically sheltered chick who's at once a coward and shows flashes of murderous ability.

Maybe having a dead brother'll force Michelle into survival mode for good.

Athena sniffs. Glances out the driver's side window.

Millipedes fat as filled sleeping bags and as long as buses chew on decaying grey plant matter near the side of the road. Sunlight bounces off their shiny segmented exoskeletons. Farther up the steep inclines are more legs. Scuttling. Insects Athena can't quite see that fight with their mammalian counterparts. Bears. Coyotes. Mountain lions. Bighorn sheep. Those critters in combat on much more equal footing since natural selection's taken a backseat to rampant mutation and unexplained growth.

Athena thumbs the screw top from a slim pint bottle of whiskey in her cup holder under the shifter. The label's long since eroded away, but it tastes like Wild Turkey.

She thinks: *I am strong. I am death. I am the absence of forgiveness. There is no poetry for me, for I am that. Strength. Death. The absence of forgiveness.*

She thinks: *I am maybe a little, tiny bit tipsy.*

Michelle squirms in her seat. Probably wants to saying something about Athena drinking and driving. Keeps her mouth shut.

Doesn't mean she doesn't have a point.

Be a shame to roll the car at this point.

Do something dumb on account of whiskey feeling like the best medicine.

Not like she got any rest between riding the rails and now.

Stupid Traker fucks and their child army.

Athena grunts. Pulls into one of the many abandoned towns that sit at the feet of the mountains. No name she can see. Not even really a town. A collection of buildings west of a titanic Walmart Supercenter.

She ignores the larger stores. Ignores the remains of a hotel. Too hard to secure. Be it from bugs or bandits.

Instead, she pulls into an area that looks like it used to be for utilities or public works. A big beige concrete and asphalt deal with a squat, eight-door garage.

Athena halts the Hellcat. Licks her lips. Waits a minute to see if some bunch of assholes wanna charge out. Make trouble.

Nothing.

She squints. Casts her eyes around. Doesn't seem like anyone or anything has been here for a while.

Which is fine by her.

She grabs another shotgun from the trunk. Remington 887 pump with a short barrel. Figures Michelle should use the sawed-off so the pregnant chick doesn't need to aim so much.

Athena nods to Michelle as she passes the passenger side of the Hellcat. Checks what seems to be the main entrance.

Door won't budge.

She kicks it.

Still won't budge.

Athena cracks her neck. "Fuck it." She punches a hole through the lock with the Remington. *Then* kicks it in.

She tucks the Remington against her shoulder. Steps sideways into the squat beige garage. Light filters in through a few thin rectangular windows high up from the ground. The place stuck in perpetual twilight.

Empty shelves where tools and supplies used to go stand as silent sentinels. Cobwebs hang from long-dead fluorescent tubes.

Vacant vehicle bays wait as well. And tools she doesn't need. Fuel canisters that ain't good anymore to run in a vehicle. Probably. But they might go boom with some encouragement.

Athena cocks an eye at the whole space. She whistles. "Hell*oooo.* Anybody home?" Ain't really any place for folks to hide except a spot near the far end. Some back room.

She marches toward it.

Keeps the gun up.

Cracked concrete crunches under Athena's boots. She passes between streams of light and shadow. Pauses outside the dark far doorway.

She thought it was some funky back room, but it's not.

There are stairs heading down. Into a black, sunless basement.

Athena sucks her teeth. Can't think of anything *good* that'd be down there. But she sure as shit ain't napping here without securing the building.

She turns around. Rummages through the main area with a bit more care. Doesn't find a flashlight but does end up with a half-dozen red road flares.

They'll do.

She stuffs five into her jacket pockets. Sparks the sixth. Winces as the acrid fumes pummel her nostrils.

Athena marches back to the top of the stairs. Holds the flare up. Watches for movement below. Now cast in a red-pink glow.

Nothing.

Just the noise of the chemicals in the flare sputtering. Hissing.

She struggles to balance the weight of the shotgun with her right hand. Muscles weak and shaky. Bullet wounds and combat injuries nowhere near healed.

Athena licks her lips. Tosses the flare down into the darkness. Repositions the shotgun with both hands. Waits. Watches.

There, in the glow, something does move.

A curious thin appendage. Spindly. Pointed. With thin bristles toward the end.

Spider leg.

It pokes the flare. Jerks back from the heat.

The whole of the thing peeks around the corner of the stairwell. Fuzzy body the size of a cougar. Sparks of light glisten in the circle of eyes around its hirsute head.

Athena sneers. "Hi there, you furry fuck."

She pulls the trigger.

Buckshot pounds the arachnid's face. Pellets shred its mandibles. Its eyes. The goo and pus-colored gore of its insides splash against the basement floor.

Athena racks the Remington's pump. A spent shell casing clacks on the concrete.

She watches. Waits.

Doesn't wanna see more legs scuttle over to investigate, but here they come.

"Furry fuck was a momma," Athena mutters.

Dozens and dozens of similarly spindly legs attached to cat-sized bodies scramble to investigate the carcass of the momma spider. The walls of the stairwell come alive with hundreds of thin shadows outlined by red. An insane puppet show.

The baby bugs don't seem interested in adventuring beyond the splattered body.

Not yet, anyway.

Athena weighs her options. Keeps the shotgun trained on the spiderlings.

She storms back. Kicks fuel cans till she finds two with sloshing fluid inside. Athena slings the shotgun over her shoulder. Shoves a flare into the mouth of each one. Carries em to the top of the stairs. Lights the chemical sticks. Hurls the gas canisters into the mass of creepy-crawly monsters.

One is squished.

The others scatter.

Athena shoots down. At the cans. Plastic and metal rupture from the 12-gauge blast. Fire gushes. Yellow and orange tongues of flame lick out.

Spiderlings scream. Squeal. They tumble away. Burning legs a blur of frenzied fire.

The second can goes up. More heat chases the arachnids.

More shadows paint the walls. Bulbous shapes.

Athena thinks: *Egg sacs.*

Thinks: *Fuck this.*

She grabs more fuel cans. Chucks em down into the fire. Then beats a hasty retreat to the Hellcat.

Michelle looks up at her. Eyebrows arched.

Athena shakes her head. "Place fuckin crawls." She starts the big Dodge. Peels outta the lot as smoke fills the sky. There's a *boom*. Another and another. Fire joins the smoke and envelopes the building.

Michelle cranes her neck to watch the inferno behind.

The Hellcat driver speeds em away from the blaze. Doesn't even wanna stay in this town. The smoke will end up attracting some dumb motherfucker. And the warmth might attract more insects.

She speeds off. Pushes on about ten miles farther west. Till she spies a cabin tucked up at the tree line away from the highway.

Athena parks the Hellcat behind it to hide the vehicle. Checks the place out. Guesses it was some rich asshole's skiing lodge back when anyone gave a damn about that kind of thing.

There're poles. Equipment. Tattered guides. Down jackets.

She finds neither bug nor beast.

And after getting Michelle inside, she plants her ass on a rickety chair on the porch. Bottle of whiskey in one hand. Smoldering cigarette in the other.

She looks out across the valley. At the mountaintops that surround her personal, nightmarish adventure. At the Colorado River that churns below. The trees that bend and sway.

Athena smokes.

Thinks: *Yeah. Humanity's done, but I've got a helluva view.*

2.

Michelle shakes Athena awake.

The Hellcat driver sneers. Stares at the pregnant woman with confusion and contempt. She's about ready to scream at the young brunette. Throw a punch. Hit the chick with an empty whiskey bottle.

But Michelle tucks a single finger to her lips.

Shhh.

Athena follows the pregnant woman's finger as it points outside.

There's a shape out there in the evening's dying light. Or the suggestion of one. A moving shadow.

Can't tell what it is.

Man or monster.

Athena's vision is still kinda blurry and fucked up from sleep and drinking. And blood loss. And coming down from the drugs. And from all the fuckin bullets she's taken in the last twenty-four hours.

She rubs her face. Pulls her Springfield Armory .45 from its holster. Goes for the sawed-off double-barrel too, but Michelle's already appropriated it.

Good for her.

Chick's showing some initiative.

Michelle points up. Toward the second floor. Unspoken question being: *Can we get a better angle up there?*

Athena nods. Crawls out from under the small avalanche of skiing parkas she used for bedding. Quiet. She gestures for Michelle to move her butt.

They both make their way to the stairs. Creep along. Step by step.

Athena moves herself along with her knees and elbows. Wants to stay low in case there's some cocksucker out there with a rifle.

She snaps her fingers. Points to the top of the stairs. Tells Michelle without words to guard that spot.

The pregnant brunette gets it. Stands vigilant.

Athena finds a window. Peers out. Down.

She sees the shape. Big lumbering thing.

Her first thought is: *A fuckin bear?*

At least it won't steal the Dodge.

Which isn't to say the big bastard won't up and *destroy* the car.

The animal down there. . .Athena recognizes it as a bear. A black bear, specifically. But like everything else now, it's a bit wrong. Twisted. Larger than it should be and with some kinda yellow and red fungus or growths all over it.

Tumors, maybe.

The bloated things wiggle. Jiggle. Drip.

Makes Athena curious about what the local fauna has actually turned into since the germ effectively removed humanity from the top of the food chain.

On the other hand, she'd love it if the mutant bear would just fuck off. Trundle away to some *other* cabin in the woods.

Issue one is: damned thing probably smells all the supplies in the trunk. The way it's sniffing around the Hellcat. Got a nose for meat and sweets.

Issue two is: damned thing probably smells tasty human meat in the form of a middle-aged leather momma and a preggo chick.

Issue three is: Athena doesn't have a single way of dealing with this awful thing. M79 grenade launcher is still in the trunk. A .45 slug doesn't do much except piss a beast like a bear off. It ain't a hunting round.

It ain't a hunting round versus your *standard* bear.

This? The mutant?

Yeah. Athena wants the grenade launcher.

But she needs to get *to* the grenade launcher.

The Hellcat driver lights a cigarette. Checks the room she's in. Been raided already. Not a lot left. But.

But. . . .

There are a few empty glass bottles. One Snapple. Another that had been a vase at some point.

Athena plucks up both. Scuttles back to Michelle. Hisses: "You piss yet?"

Michelle whispers: "Are you kidding?"

Athena hands her the Snapple bottle. "Squirt what you can inside. It's a big goddamn fuckoff bear. I gotta give it something to sniff other than the car." She arches her eyebrows. Blows smoke. "Tinkle, tinkle little star."

Michelle groans. "Christ."

"Least we ain't getting shot at."

Both women dump their bladders.

Athena readjusts her leathers. Hoists two warm containers of urine. Plugs the openings with torn scraps of parka and fabric so they don't spill all over the damn place.

She goes back to the window. Leans out.

The bear freak is still milling around the Hellcat. Its big weird nose sniffs. Scarred muzzle shakes and slobbers. It huffs and chuffs.

Athena takes aim with the piss-filled Snapple bottle. The weight about that of a baseball. Her target is a tree about fifty feet away. She hurls it. Happy to get the throw off without getting pee on herself.

The bottle sails. Tumbles when it hits a small branch. Finally smashes against its target.

Urine *pitter patters* on the ground.

The bear stops. Whips around at the noise. Rears up on its hind legs. Sniffs. Stomps back down on all fours. Then trundles with some caution in the direction of the pee tree.

Athena flaps her hands at Michelle. *Go go.*

The two make their way back downstairs. Quiet as they can. They leave nothing behind except a few empty cans of Chef Boyardee and a mostly-drunk bottle of whiskey.

Athena clicks the key fob in her jacket pocket. Unlocks the Hellcat as they move toward it. She squints at the bear freak. Mutant bastard still enamored with the stench of the pregnant woman's piss. Maybe the hormones in the fluid.

That's fine.

Athena slides behind the wheel.

Michelle takes the passenger seat.

Athena watches the bear in her side mirror. Starts the Hellcat. The V8 roars to life.

The bear takes notice. Rears up again to see what this new animal might be. Then continues its urine investigation.

The Hellcat driver figures: *fuck it.*

If the bear doesn't give a damn, why should she?

Plus, Athena doesn't remember how many 40mm grenades she got from those Rocky Rangers at the camp. Better to save em for targets that *deserve* it. Not some wild animal.

Athena lights a cigarette. Breathes deep. Winces at the pain in her chest.

The pain tells her that her time is short.

Journey's close to over.

Suits Athena.

Just means getting to the redwoods has a new sense of urgency about it.

Athena guns the Hellcat. Puts em on I-70 West.

She's still kinda fucked up. Hungover. Groggy. So she keeps the speed reasonable. Scans the little towns for some place they can stop that ain't just in the middle of the road. Put food in their bellies without the threat of bears or goddamn asshole spiders.

Harder than one might think.

Respite comes in the form of a park. Some campground called Island Acres.

The name doesn't make a lick of sense to Athena. It ain't an island. Just a lumpy offshoot of dirt and trees and trails and ponds that the Colorado River bends and heads south around.

But whatever.

It's quiet. No signs of anything that wants to eat em. It's open. So Athena doesn't need to worry about one of those wants-to-eat-me things sneaking up on em.

It'll do.

The Hellcat glides along a straightaway that's flanked by large ponds. Passed the welcome center for this River State Park "Island" bullshit.

Full dark soon.

Inky black above the mountains already hinting at its supremacy.

And as usual, Athena would rather not be on the road. Headlights of the Hellcat declaring her position every step of the way.

Athena coughs as she pulls the Hellcat around. Around another pond up to another tourist center.

She parks her car near a random camping spot. One populated by a family skeletal remains and the pieces of a life long lost. A decrepit trailer that musta been towed here by a truck or something.

Athena sees stones organized around a fire pit. Photos. Thinks in her mind about a dinner unfinished. Some celebration of why any family would be here.

Not that it ain't pretty.

Picturesque, even.

Athena keeps her sawed-off shotgun up. Barges into that small camping trailer. Checks it.

Clear.

Not like there's much room for anyone to hide.

She ushers her sole remaining bargaining chip inside. Michelle. Snaps at a nearby bed. Says, "Rest. Eat." Darkness has nearly taken over outside.

Athena waits. Near the Hellcat. Casts her eyes around.

Without the light pollution, you can see everything.

The sky is so bright.

Stars. Comets. Our place in the backwater of this spiral galaxy.

Milk with specks in the black sky.

Athena lights a cigarette. Hears movement nearby.

She hopes it ain't a bear, but it might be.

She pops the trunk. Grabs the chopped-down M79. Loads a 40mm shell in the chamber. Tucks another into her jacket pocket.

Feet.

She hears feet running toward her.

Paws on dirt. Punching the ground.

Not heavy steps. Quick. Light. In a gallop.

She pulls her .45.

Whatever kinda critter it is, she figures it's gotta be kinda small if it's moving that fast. Her Springfield Armory 1911 should do the job. If need be.

She keeps her back to the Hellcat. Gun up. Grenade launcher slung over her shoulder if the sound brings more trouble.

And then. . . .

A dog of some kind runs and stops about ten feet away. Eyes bright in the Hellcat's headlights. Its furry butt on the ground.

The thing itself a mix between Greyhound and. . .hair. Also huge. Got that Greyhound shape—slender with an oversized ribcage and narrow snout—but it's massive and has long fur.

Athena cocks her head at the dog. Keeps the pistol aimed. "I have no idea what you are." She wracks her brain.

She sees its matted fur. Eager eyes. Not starvation, but hunger. The particular leanness that brings.

There's a cut on its back left leg. The flesh there open. A fuzzy flap hangs.

Metal underneath.

Chrome.

Athena grunts. "Frankie or some other bugfuck genius in the wastes?" She eyeballs the pooch. "Could you have made it this far? All the way from that nuke plant in Ohio. . . ."

Whine.

"I don't really need a pet. Already got a tag-along." Athena keeps her .45 on the dog. "Fuck makes you special?"

Bark.

"Tough little—" Athena dips her head from side to side. "—You're tough as nails, is that your thing? Whatever he was doing to you, you made it. Got all the way here. Killing your way west. I can respect that. . .Fuckin Frankie—"

Whine.

"What? Frankie?" Athena lifts the leathers around her right leg. Shows some chrome. "He would have something weird like you running around."

Whine.

"Well, I killed that motherfucker, so—"

Bark.

"Yeah, I know. 'Asshole' doesn't begin to cover it." Athena holsters her pistol. Pops the Dodge's trunk. Snaps her fingers— which gets the dog to trot over to her.

Big beast of a canine trots to her. Stands as tall as her waist. Sniffs her right foot. Where she ain't human anymore.

She says, "Fresh meat ain't really on the menu. Shit's probably as radioactive as the rest of us are. And I sure as hell ain't gonna waste space with dog food. But. . . ." Athena rummages through the supplies. Closes her fingers around a can of Campbell's Chunky Hearty Beef Barely. Shows it to the dog. Says, "I mean, this is basically dog food, right?"

Bark bark.

Athena pulls the tab at the top of the can. Cracks the Campbell's open.

The dog's ears perk up when it smells the chow. It does a little dance. Taps its front paws against the ground. Whines a little.

"Yeah, yeah." She sets the open tin in front of it. "Eating outta the can is good enough for us so it's gonna have to be good enough for you too."

The dog doesn't care. It dips its snout into the food. Licks. Slobbers.

Athena crosses her arms. Stares at the wasteland canine. "What'm I supposed to call you?"

The dog continues to eat. Oblivious to the Hellcat driver's question. And, Athena thinks, it probably doesn't care *what* she ends up naming it anyway.

She squats while the dog chows down. Sees the cock at its crotch. Grunts.

"Given how things go out here, you might split open and unleash some nightmare." Athena sniffs. "But other than that you seem okay."

She watches the dog finish his meal. Thinks. "Wasn't too long ago, I was shooting your friends. Killing pups. Sticking your kin in an oven for a few days." She cocks an eye at the dog. "Haven't had jerky in a while, but it'd be fucked up if I fed you that, huh?" Athena chuckles. "Dog meat." She snaps her fingers.

The dog runs to her side.

Athena rubs it behind the ears.

She says, "You're Dogmeat."

Bark bark.

"Yeah." Athena smirks. "Wanna go kill a cougar? A *bear?*" She fingers the grenade launcher on her back. "Lots of meat on those."

A scream sounds from Michelle's throat in the camping trailer.

Michelle.

Athena grips the .45 on her leg. Breaks into wide-legged a run. Linebacker at full-tilt.

If Michelle dies, the baby dies. If the baby dies, there goes Athena's best card to play against whoever the fuck she meets in California.

She's always figured whatever mewling mess Michelle managed to squeeze out would be a meal ticket. Free pass.

Healthy baby. Right here. You gimme gas and grub, I give you the kid.

Athena charges through the door to the trailer. Sees Michelle in the pale blue light of a Coleman lantern in the back on a ratty bed. The pregnant woman shrieks. Holds her belly.

Michelle can't talk. It's all grunts and screams. Then mostly cursing. A furrowed brow and sweat. "Fuck. *Fuck.*" She rocks from side to side. "It hurts." She coughs. "*The baby.*"

Dogmeat barks.

Athena spreads her hands. "The baby fuckin *what?* What am I supposed to do here?" Memories of the child Athena and David never got to have flash across her mind. The fullness of family becomes empty. Lonely. Cancer and life and a uterus that didn't want to allow life. *"What the fuck am I supposed to do here?"*

Michelle groans. Breathes at a rapid pace.

Athena balls her hand into a fist. Wants to punch Michelle. Confusion and the feeling of helplessness translates into anger.

Fuck your youth. Fuck your health. Fuck your beauty. Fuck your ability to have a child.

She holds herself.

Dogmeat howls.

Michelle's rapid breathing slows. "False. . .false alarm. It's the, uh, shit. I don't remember what Mark called em. My body thinks the baby is ready to come out but it isn't quite." Michelle tilts her head back. "Contractions."

Athena huffs.

Dogmeat sits on his haunches.

Michelle looks up. "Nice fuckin Borzoi, by the way."

Athena shifts her weight from one foot to the other. "Fuck is a boar-zoy."

"That." Michelle points with a limp finger. Right at Dogmeat. "Russian wolfhound." She smirks. Sweat drips from her.

Athena glances at Dogmeat. Says, "You know dogs always die in stories like this, right? They're a cheap plot device to emotionally impact readers."

Dogmeat whines.

Athena laughs. "Relax, I'm just fuckin with you.

"We're *all* gonna die."

Michelle nods as she lies back down. "Great. Just great."

3.

Dogmeat yawns next to the Hellcat. The pooch and his paws in the dirt. The dust. Morning sun bounces off his white and apricot fur.

Athena's leathers squeak as she reaches into a pocket. Produces the first cigarette she'll punish her body with today.

She smokes. Talks to the dog. "Still here, huh?"

Dogmeat licks his lips. Pants. Keeps his ass planted.

"Dunno what your fuckin deal is, but all right." She eyeballs the Hellcat's backseat. "You're big but you oughtta fit in there. No point in making you run more."

She goes to the car's trunk for breakfast.

Now the dog's up and interested.

Athena grabs a can of stew for herself. More beef soup for the dog. She does a quick count of the remaining cans.

Having an extra mouth around ain't the greatest thing in the world.

Be worse when Michelle pops out her kid.

It's all gonna necessitate more stopping. More scavenging.

Athena puffs her cheeks. Blows air and smoke out. Cracks a can for Dogmeat. One for herself. She spoons stew into her mouth between pulls from the cigarette. Looks around at the mountains in the cold morning air. "If I was smart, I'd just fuckin go."

She shivers. "I'd also get myself a warmer jacket." Athena sniffs. Flicks her cigarette away. Shoves the remainder of the stew down her gullet. Chucks the can into the circle of stones that makes up the fire pit.

The tin hits a stack of bones that might've been a mom or a dad or a son or a daughter or. . .who gives a shit.

Athena plucks up a package of sanitary wipes. The sawed-off shotgun.

She struts to the trailer door. Bangs on it with the 12-gauge barrel. "Woman. Come watch the car. My turn for four walls."

Athena rests her head against the side of the trailer. Brain under her short-cropped blonde hair throbbing from booze and stress. She snaps her fingers at Dogmeat.

The borzoi halts. Sits.

Athena nods with some respect. "Not bad, fur ball."

Michelle wanders outta the trailer. Wrapped in a blanket. The pregnant brunette blinks in the morning light. Not moving too fast.

Athena hands her the shotgun. Nods to the open trunk of the Hellcat. "Breakfast." Nods to Dogmeat. "He seems okay."

Michelle exhales through her nose. Eyes the pooch. Reaches a tentative hand to the canine's snout.

Dogmeat stands. Sniffs. Leans against her in apparent desperate need of petting.

Athena grunts. Heads inside. She closes the door tight behind her. Not cuz she's ashamed of what's under all the leather, but Athena hates the idea some weirdo jerk in the weeds might be whacking it to her body.

So she strips down. Rubs all the tired. Sore. Bloody. Bruised parts of her. Light crimson comes away from the bullet holes. Gashes. Cuts that would join her numerous other scars in time if she wasn't dead-set on dying.

Only "mirror" in the damn trailer is a single shard that hangs like a rotten shingle. She can't look at herself. Not fully. Only in fragments.

Athena tosses the used sanitary wipes. Gets dressed. Goes back outside.

Michelle's sitting in the passenger seat. Door open. She's still wrapped in the big blanket. Crank radio in her lap. Dogmeat rests at her feet.

Athena grunts. "Rocky Rangers said radio's all fuckaroo here in the mountains."

Michelle shrugs. She tucks herself into the car fully. Closes the door.

Athena walks to the driver's side. Opens the back door. Snaps her fingers.

Dogmeat shoots up. Tail wagging with such enthusiasm it's like a prop on an airplane. He hops into the backseat. Spins around once. Twice. Finally plops down. Licks his chops and stares at Athena. His face carries an expression of: *Yeah, okay. Let's go.*

The Hellcat driver licks her own lips. Nods. Starts the car and rolls the Dodge around to the welcome center at the entrance/

exit to the camp grounds. She struts up to a map tacked to the side of the building. Follows I-70 with her finger.

There's a town nearby. Palisade. Which's just outside the Rockies. Decent-sized, too. Makes Athena a bit anxious.

Not as anxious as the comparative enormity of Grand Junction, though.

She rubs her forehead. Thinks: *Fuck.*

There ain't any route they can take to avoid the sudden flourish of what was once civilization. And the danger the city and suburbs represent is obvious. Raiders. Cultists. Loons like Frankie. Maybe that "Western Devil" the Trakers seemed spooked by.

What she doesn't want is to come across some barricade on the highway. A barrier between her and California she can't drive through.

She'd rather contend with mutant bears.

Athena considers the options.

Decides: *Fuck it.*

She'll spend the ammo if she has to. The grenades. And Michelle can do some damage with the 12-gauge.

Athena puts em back on the road.

Michelle watches her. Says, "Problem?"

Athena shakes her head. "Just keep that shotgun ready."

They burn rubber. Beige rocky cliff face to their right. Wide expanse of fields and green to their left. Cracked asphalt under em.

Palisade comes and goes without incident.

Athena shifts in her seat as they clear most of the mountains.

The area around em gets flatter. The grey of previous vegetation is sprinkled by hints of green. Acres of ranchland stand vacant and unused.

Michelle scans the dial on her radio. She's rewarded with an endless stream of static.

Athena keeps her grip on the wheel tight. Eyes forward.

Then the static on the radio cuts out. It's replaced by a sudden burst of speech. "This is Sergeant Major Oliver Bradley of the New California Republic—"

Athena arches her eyebrows.

"—My troopers and I are pinned down by raiders at the Grand Junction airport. We have been so for over a day now. Our cargo plane was damaged by enemy fire. We need the time and the tools to repair it. This is a call for support from any nearby road runners or militias. You will be handsomely rewarded for any assistance provided. Message repeats. . . ."

Michelle turns to Athena.

Athena grunts. "Sounds thin."

"There's that part about a 'reward,' though."

"They gonna reward us like Frankie? Or the Trakers?"

Dogmeat whines in the backseat.

Michelle shrugs. "Given my motherfuckin situation—and yours—the idea of a plane that can get us to California seems worth investigating. Y'know, with a quickness."

Athena takes a deep breath. Winces.

The pregnant girl ain't wrong.

An explosion blooms off to the far right. A small flash of fire under a much larger cloud of smoke and dirt inside a massive, fenced-off area.

Athena figures she's found the airport.

She pulls the Hellcat off to the side of the road. Steps out. Raises her busted binoculars to her eyes. She scans the rocky land outside the airport. One long tarmac to her right. The main landing strip north of that. A lotta buildings in between.

From where she stands on I-70, she counts seven vehicles kicking up dust. A mix of pickups and SUVs. Which seems about on-par for every goddamn group of assholes she's come across.

Another explosion rips through the air. This one near—but missing—the raider trucks.

Athena considers what she's seeing. Guesses it's more likely that an organized military force like the California Republic is gonna have boom-booms than some ragtag raider cocksuckers.

Then again, those raider bastards managed to force a cargo plane to land.

So. . . .

Who knows.

She pops the Hellcat's trunk. Examines her options. Not great. No real long-range weapons. She misses her scoped Remington 700 rifle badly. If she could get on top of a nearby building, sending some .300 WinMag rounds into the skulls of some scum would be a relative pleasure.

Instead, she'll bring the fight to them.

Athena grabs a satchel of 40mm grenades. Slings it over her injured shoulder. She guns the Dodge's V8. Charges down I-70. Takes the off ramp that brings her north toward the airport.

She's gonna drive right up the main entrance.

Right up their taints.

Athena mutters to herself. Whispers. Grumbles. Thinks: *I am strong. I am death. I am the absence of forgiveness.*

She lights a cigarette. Checks the chamber of the M79 launcher. The thumper in her lap.

Michelle does the same for the sawed-off shotgun.

They blow by a smattering of hotels and gas stations and eateries on Horizon Drive. The massive warehouses for the airport loom ahead. Off to their right. Horizon becomes Eagle. The rusted bodies of two old fighter jets wait on struts over a roundabout.

Ahead is the airport itself.

A couple trucks turned sideways block the entrance. They form a barricade. Gunners stand on the flatbeds. Heavy weapons in their hands.

Athena sees insignia on the sides of the trucks. Skull and bones where the bones are wrenches. She sneers.

Iron Cross.

Sonuvabitch.

They turn to face the roar of the Hellcat.

Michelle readies her 12-gauge.

Athena tilts the grenade launcher out her window with her left hand. The M79 *thump*s.

The explosive round goes boom between the two trucks. Fire and shrapnel tear through the vehicles and the Iron Cross bastards on guard. Gas tanks in the trucks go up in secondary explosions. Burning wrecks lift off the ground for a split second until gravity brings em down again onto the messy carcasses of dead, crispy raiders.

Athena cuts the wheel. Brings the Hellcat to a skidding stop. She waits. Listens for the sounds of gunfire. Combat.

Off to the right still.

The Hellcat shoots off. Follows the pavement. Athena slides up the metal shutters across the windshield. Rams through the security gate ahead. The Dodge's bullbar makes short work of the chain link fence.

A heartbeat later, they're burning rubber under the massive wings of FedEx cargo planes. Flying between shuttled, long-dead aircraft. Those dumb little carts luggage handlers use on the tarmac.

Athena pulls a hard right. Stomps the gas. The Hellcat roars down the runway. Hits fifty. Sixty. Seventy.

The small skeletons of single-prop planes and private jets become a blur around em.

She sees a fat bird ahead. At the end of the tarmac. A military C-130 variant in matte grey. One of its engines seems to be fucked up. One of the props tilted at a bad angle. Wires hanging and the casing split.

The rear loading ramp is down. Guarded by a handful of people in camouflage gear. A couple machine gun turrets tucked up against sandbags. All apparently watching the carnage taking place some distance away.

Athena thinks: *Holy fuckballs, they've got a working cargo plane.*

She turns the car right. Before she gets too close to the guards at the C-130. She sees more of em farther out in the dirt in defensive positions. More guns on swivels. The cover there mostly consisting of small divots in the ground.

Which is to say: the cover is worth fuckall.

Especially when you take the dozen or so New California Republic bodies into account.

Athena keeps to a service road that runs south. Parallel to the fighting. High-caliber weaponry goes *budda budda budda.*

She hits the brakes. Takes aim at an Iron Cross truck about to strafe the soldiers under fire.

Thump.

The shell sails. Splashes fire across the front of the truck. It blows a hole through the cab. Again ignites the gas tank. Flames engulf the entire vehicle. The gunner in the bed flails. Stumbles for a moment. Then becomes a burning mound of clothes and flesh and hair.

Rounds of ammunition pop off in the wreckage.

Athena looks across the landscape to the pinned soldiers. Smokes. Reloads the grenade launcher. Offers em a weak thumbs-up—mostly in the hopes they don't fuck this up and shoot at her.

One of the NCR troopers waves.

That's good enough for Athena.

She pushes farther south. Rugged tires of the Hellcat kicking up plenty of dirt and stone. Traction ain't so great. But she'd rather be on the move.

Another hefty pickup makes a beeline for the Hellcat. Grill burdened by a variety of skulls. Asshole in the truck bed taking wild potshots with a carbine.

Athena barks at Michelle. "I'm gonna get you side by side with this limp dick."

Michelle nods.

Athena taps the brakes. Slows to turn harder than the truck. Lets the Iron Cross pukes overshoot her. Then floors it to catch up.

The truck's gunner adjusts his aim. Fires a few rounds. Pangs the door on Michelle's side.

She snaps the shotgun up. Shreds the gunner's guts with a load of pellets. Changes targets. Dumps the second shell of buckshot into the truck's front left tire. Ruins the rubber there.

The truck slams to a stop when the bare metal of the wheel there embeds itself in the ground. The front end faceplants. The driver is smashed to a bloody pulp. The rear kicks up. Catapults the carcass of the gunner out.

Dogmeat barks.

Athena nods.

Michelle drops the shotgun. Doesn't reload but retrieves the other pump scattergun so she can keep shooting at other incoming baddies—an SUV and a truck.

They try to sandwich the Hellcat. SUV on the left. Truck on the right.

Michelle shatters one of the truck's side windows as it rushes up on em. Jerks back inside the Dodge when the big Ford slams into the Hellcat's side. She racks the slide. Ejects a shell. Waits until Athena jukes away. Fires again but hits nothing.

Athena pulls her Springfield .45 and dumps three rounds into the side door of the SUV as it rams her from the right. Hopes the bullets can plow through the metal there and hit the driver.

No dice.

And the SUV's too close for an M79 shell to arm itself.

One of the rear doors on the SUV flies open. A raider leans out. Throws himself on top of the Hellcat.

Michelle unloads on the truck.

The SUV and the truck close in again.

Athena watches the vehicles' front wheels. Waits for em to tilt inward toward her path.

They do.

At the same time.

Athena stomp and holds the brakes. She and Michelle are thrown forward. Their dig into their flesh. Michelle wails at the sudden pressure on her midsection. Dogmeat unceremoniously flops onto the floor in the back seat.

The raider on the roof tumbles onto the hood. Grips it there with a strained face.

The SUV and the truck collide ahead. They bounce off each other with metallic screeches.

Athena throws the Hellcat into reverse. Pulls back till she thinks she's got the right distance. Stops the car. Steps out.

The Iron Cross raider scrambles toward her on the hood.

She aims her .45 at his balls. "Don't touch the fuckin—"

Dogmeat gallops from the backseat. Jumps and pins him to the ground. The borzoi's jaw firmly clamped around the raider's neck. Growls turn to gurgles in the spigot of blood.

Athena grunts. Turns. Raises the grenade launcher. Sends a shell downrange.

It explodes.

Just not where she wants it too.

Damn thing falls short.

Blows up nothing but dirt.

The truck and the SUV get their shit together. Readjust their trajectories. Spin their tires. Gun their engines.

Several thousand pounds bear down on her.

Athena reloads. Fast. Every second those bastards keep moving, keep closing the gap, the less likely it is the grenade will arm.

Michelle makes her presence known with a shotgun blast. The pellets from each round scrape and crack the tarnished metal and skulls and glass of the raider vehicles.

The grenade launcher in Athena's hands *thump*s.

The shell soars.

Impacts on the grill of the SUV. Chews up the engine. Sends the SUV on a flaming path of doom right into the truck. They collide again. With far more violence. The gas tanks rupture. Spill fire and thunder.

Each one comes to a slow sad flaming halt. The raider occupants scream as their skin cooks. They beat their hands against doors and windows.

Athena arches her eyebrows at Michelle.

The pregnant woman blinks. Smirks. "Fuck em, let em cook."

Dogmeat licks his bloody chops. Body of the Iron Cross goon unmoving.

Athena reloads. Spins on her boot heels. Checks for any remaining raiders.

There's one smoldering heap of an SUV. Riddled with bullet holes. Must've been taken out by the NCR while Athena and Michelle were in combat.

Two other trucks remain active. One waits out by the far southern end of the parallel tarmac. Maybe some asshole in charge, leading from the rear like cowards in command tend to. Or a guy just waiting to bug out and report to. . .whoever.

The other truck makes a beeline for the Hellcat. A suicide charge. Gunner in the bed screaming and firing his machine gun. The skulls on the hood and grill all bony smiles.

Athena digs into her satchel for a fresh 40mm grenade.

Comes up empty.

Fuck.

Should've kept moving.

Athena slings the M79. Pulls her pistol. Dumps the rest of her mag into the windshield of the charging truck. Spider webs appear in the glass.

But the trucks charges on.

The gunner in back rests the bipod of his light machine gun on the roof of the truck cab. He peppers the dirt around the Hellcat with bullets. A few rounds slam into the Dodge's side.

Dogmeat bolts. The pooch smart enough to know this ain't the place to be.

Athena takes cover. Shouts at Michelle to do the same. She drops the spent mag from her 1911. Pops in a fresh one. Fires from over the hood of the Hellcat.

She hears footsteps behind her. Whirls and puts the barrel of her Springfield Armory in an NCR soldier's face.

He holds up a hand. Guy about her age. Blue eyes surrounded by hair and a beard that's gone grey from genetics or stress. His fatigues are worn and torn. Boots beat to hell. He's got a badge and a bronze star on his chest.

Greybeard doesn't say anything. Just puts his back to the Hellcat. Tugs a fat two-foot tube from its place at his shoulder. Yanks the rear and extends the launcher.

Athena recognizes it from war movies. An M72 LAW.

The Iron Cross truck is less than a hundred feet away now.

Greybeard stands. Lays the tube over his shoulder. Aims. Fires.

A rocket speeds away with a crack and a puff of smoke. Streaks for the truck on its own glorious suicide mission.

The Iron Cross driver tries to juke the truck. He succeeds only in turning the vehicle sideways.

The rocket explodes on the passenger door. Breaks the truck in half. Two halves connected by a few sinews of metal. They roll and burn. Come to a wobbly grinding halt about thirty feet from the Hellcat.

Athena watches. Sniffs. Spits. She takes a few deep breaths.

The NCR soldier eyeballs her. Nods.

She returns the gesture. Then shouts. "Michelle?" Runs around the front of her car. She sees the prone shape of the pregnant brunette on the ground. A dirty, dusty pool of blood near her neck.

Michelle looks up to Athena. Hand clamped at her throat. Eyes aware but fading.

Dogmeat trots back to the Dodge. Sits patiently near Athena and Michelle. Whines.

Athena snaps her fingers at Greybeard. "I need a medic. *Right the fuck now.*" She drops to her knees. Grabs a rag from inside the Hellcat's open passenger side. She pushes Michelle's hand away from the wound. Sees the mean, bleeding trough that's been carved through the pregnant woman's neck by a raider bullet. Presses the rag hard there. Holds it as it grows red. Sticky.

She shouts again: "*I need a medic over here.*"

Michelle and Athena lock eyes. Neither speaks.

Athena casts a furious glance over her shoulder. Watches the final Iron Cross truck at the distant end of the runway turn tail. The cowards flee. Leave only the dead, the smoking husks of their vehicles and trails of dust behind.

She thinks to herself: *I am the absence of forgiveness.*

4.

Athena leans against the Hellcat. Now parked near the damaged C-130.

Her own machine wounded badly enough that it hurts her heart. Fresh bullet holes and scratches. She knows the thing'll run till it's Swiss cheese. Just hates to see the Dodge in this kinda shape.

Dogmeat lies near her feet. The big long-haired canine flopped on his side. Panting. Seemingly asleep.

She lights a cigarette. Lifts an open bottle of Wild Turkey to her lips.

The ten remaining NCR troopers pull their armaments back to the cargo on the tarmac. Mounted weapons. A couple .50-caliber Brownings protected by sandbags. M249 light machine guns.

Those sandbags and machine guns protect the open ramp of the C-130. Plus whatever's inside—like Michelle.

The pregnant woman being tended to by two doctors in the expansive cargo bay.

Athena's glad the brunette wasn't snuffed out.

Less sure, though, if it's good she's in NCR hands now. Lot harder to make a meal ticket outta the chick and her kid if whatever passes for military is taking care of her.

Greybeard walks toward Athena while she smokes. Drinks. His M4 carbine at rest on a sling across his chest.

Dogmeat stirs. Senses the visitor. Bolts upright. Watches the soldier.

Athena snaps her fingers.

Dogmeat sits.

Greybeard cocks an eye at the two of em. Says to Athena, "The girl's stable."

Athena nods. "The baby?"

"Look, neither of em are *good*, all right?" Greybeard puts his hands on his hips. "Malnutrition. And the girl *did* take a grazing shot to the neck. But they're alive. Our trauma docs are top-notch." He takes a breath. Holds his hand out. "Sergeant Major Oliver Bradley."

Athena pinches her cigarette with her lips. Tilts her head back to avoid getting smoke in her eyes. She takes Oliver's hand. Doesn't say anything else.

Oliver bites his lip. Squints at the Hellcat driver. "All right. So I'll ask: Who the hell are you?"

She blows smoke through her nose. Drops the butt of her cigarette on the ground. Mashes it with a boot heel. "Athena Kozielewski."

"Military?"

Athena shakes her head. "Mechanic."

Oliver guffaws. "A mechanic." He nods at the ground. "A. . .polish *mechanic* drives into the airport and leads a two-woman counterassault using military-grade high explosives to great effect." He looks to the Hellcat. "In a muscle car."

Athena shrugs. "Yeah. Well." She chugs her whiskey. Waits a couple beats. "You said something about a reward on the radio."

"Yeah." Oliver rubs his forehead. Frowns. "I did." He sighs. "You mind if I bury my fuckin people before I open up the market to you?"

Athena nods. "I want that woman and that baby taken care of. And I want you to remember what the both of us did for the New California Republic." She points at the man. "I ain't going anywhere. It's better I'm on your side than against it."

Oliver's eyebrows shoot up. "For who?" He turns. Walks back to his soldiers.

For the next four hours, Athena watches New California Republic troopers cremate their dead. It's a somber series of small ceremonies.

Each body is brought to the side of the C-130 farthest from where the carnage has taken place. Carried by two of the remaining soldiers. Bradley says a few words. The others salute. A torch-bearer sets the corpse alight.

Repeat.

Fifteen times.

Smoke blackens the sky.

Course, nobody gives a damn about the raider carcasses.

Oliver wanders back to the Hellcat. Face smeared with ash. Soot. He with a small brown vacuum-sealed package. "It's, uh, *fettucine alfredo*. Has a little flameless heater inside."

Athena nods from the driver's seat. The door open. Her sideways. Whiskey bottle in her lap. She takes the MRE. Rubs her thumb over the words printed on it. "Thanks." She juts her chin toward the burning bodies. "You do that every time? Seen it before."

Oliver takes a deep breath. "Cremation is the only way to make sure the remains aren't. . . ." He sniffs. Shakes his head. "Raiders and animals. They get to the bodies otherwise. Any organization that cares is gonna cremate their dead. Where'd you see it?"

"Trakers?" Athena cocks her head. "Railroad assholes. Well, no, the kids did it."

Oliver nods. Slow. He frowns. "The Trakers are an issue that we're aware of. Just like the Iron Cross." He turns. Points to the fifteen pillars of smoke. "The men and women who serve the New California Republic, however, do so with integrity and honor. They deserve to be remembered. Their badges and stars will be hung in the Hall of Heroes. Troopers will continue their march, knowing that the fallen did not die in vain."

"You don't need to blow smoke up my ass, pal." Athena lights a cigarette.

"And you don't need to be so cynical."

Athena takes a mouthful of whiskey into her cheeks. Swallows. Smokes. "Pretty fuckin sure I do." She reaches down. Rubs Dogmeat behind the ears. First time she's bothered to show the critter some affection.

Dogmeat yawns. Stretches. Stands. White fur around his muzzle still stained red. He takes a step toward Athena. Sits. Rests his head in her lap.

She runs her fingers through the long hair that drapes away from his neck. Says, "You ever hear of Doctor Frankie?"

"Of course. He's a key target of the Republic."

"Why?"

"We want his technology." Oliver shrugs. "If we had those kinds of tools? Equipment? We could reclaim the wastes in a fraction of the time. Frankie himself would have to be killed, of course—the man's insane—but the technology is *extremely* valuable. The robotics. The artificial intelli—"

"Yeah, well, beat you to it." Athena flaps a hand.

Oliver furrows his brow. "What does that mean, precisely?"

"I ran into one of Frankie's machines on my way west. He imprisoned me. That pregnant girl in your plane. Her now-dead brother. He did. . .nightmarish things to us. The girl won't even talk about *what* he did to her." Athena blows smoke. Rolls her tongue around in her mouth. Thinks. "I killed the motherfucker."

She remembers that "motherfucker" is a terrifyingly apt term for Frankie.

Oliver shifts his weight from one foot to the other. "That's a little hard to believe."

"Is it?" Athena takes a long pull from her cigarette. "You saw what I did here. Solved your little Iron Cross problem for you. Just me and the pregnant girl."

"That doesn't mean you took out Doctor Frankie and his machines. Our intel suggests he has an entire factory and production plant—"

Athena rolls her eyes. "Yeah. He *did*. I'm telling you the motherfucker's as dead as dog shit."

"I'm gonna have to verify that. There's no way for me to even know you actually crossed paths with Frankie." He squints at her. "Which isn't to say we didn't appreciate the help, but you asked about the reward right away. You strike me as an opportunist."

Athena grunts. Tucks her cigarette into the corner of her mouth. She snaps her fingers at Dogmeat and points to the ground nearby. The apocalypse canine obeys. Leaves her lap.

She stomps her foot down. Reaches for the cuff of her leathers at her right ankle. Rolls em up. Shows off the chrome there where flesh oughtta be.

Athena smiles.

Oliver stiffens. He snaps up his M4. Points the barrel at the Hellcat driver's head. "What the fuck is going on here? What are you?"

Athena purses her lips. "Told you. A mechanic." She blows smoke. "You wanted proof I'd seen Frankie." She points to her leg. "That look like anything some raggedy-ass wastelander could throw together in an afternoon?" She motions to Dogmeat with her cigarette. "Pooch has one too. It's one hundred percent, grade-A Frankie nightmare tech."

Oliver's hands are tight around the M4. His finger hovers above the trigger. *On* it, but not pressing. Not yet. "You're not filling me with confidence here, Hellcat."

"And I don't want a fuckin 5.56 round in my brain. What do you want from me?"

"You're human?"

Athena takes another mouthful of whiskey. Follows that with a painkiller. Finishes her cigarette. Coughs. "Meet a lotta chain-smoking, cancerous, alcoholic cyborgs these days?"

"No." His gun doesn't waver. "You killed him, you get a hold of Frankie's tech?"

Athena thinks: *Maybe blowing that whole place to hell wasn't the best idea I've ever had. And maybe that Iron Cross kid Sherlock was right. But. . . .*

She Lies. "No. Dunno what happened to it. Place was going boom while we were running away from the monsters he made."

Oliver lowers his rifle. "Damn shame."

"Really? Most folks were pretty happy after we skewered his ass."

"No, fuck the man. I'm talking about the technology, woman. *The technology.* All gone."

Athena chuckles. "All gone. Whatcha gonna do." She mouths the whiskey.

"Not gone. What we're gonna do is you're gonna join us so our technicians can check out your leg. And the girl."

"...am I?"

"You are."

Athena grunts. "This my reward?"

"Think of it as continued service." He tilts his head toward the troopers near the ramp of the C-130. The gun emplacements aimed directly at the Hellcat. "Less you'd rather be a smear."

Dogmeat growls.

Athena pats his head. Calms the canine. "I got a couple reservations."

"Let's hear em."

Athena starts the Hellcat engine. "Car goes with me."

Oliver sighs. Waits a moment. Two. "All right." He nods to his soldiers.

They clear a path.

Athena snaps her fingers. Dogmeat worms his way into the backseat of the Dodge. She drives it forward. Up the ramp into the body of the C-130. Stops it right in front of a wide dividing wall. She's surprised how fuckin big the cargo bay is.

She steps out. Keeps her hands up. Away from the 1911 on her thigh. Says to Oliver as he walks up the ramp. To the other NCR troopers: "So you've got me and the car and you wanna toy with my leg."

Oliver steps up into the cargo bay. "If you and that pregnant woman and the *dog* are what remains of Frankie's tech? Yeah. I want NCR scientists to get a look at y'all."

"Where?"

Y'all? This motherfucker just say "Y'all?"

Oliver bites his lip. "That's not information I'm ready to share." He puts a hand up. Signals to the other troopers to lower their weapons. "You said 'a couple reservations.' So what's the other, now that you got your car here."

"Wasn't a reservation." Athena cocks her eye at Oliver. "More like—" Athena pretends to juggle with her hands. "I wanted the Hellcat up with me."

"All right. Why?"

Athena shows off the key fob to the Hellcat. "The Dodge is primed to blow." She makes an explosion noise with her mouth. "You do something I don't like—" She chuckles. "Then we all go."

It's utter horseshit, but Athena sells it well enough.

She shouts, "So if *y'all* suckfucks wanna fiddle with me and the dog and the pregnant girl, all right. But you're taking us to California."

Oliver puts up a hand to the Hellcat driver. He lets his M4 fall on its sling at his side. "Athena? Hellcat. *Hellcat.*" He shakes his head. "This might come as a goddamn shock to you, but we don't. . . ." He sighs. Rubs his face. "I'm gonna apologize for the same shit that you feel the need to do. Namely, being a righteous dick." He spreads his hands. "Yeah, I threatened you. That tends to be the cost of doing business with savages. But—" He brings his hands together "—you're not a savage. You're not a violent lunatic. And I'm sorry. I really—" He laughs. Sniffs. "I really do not want you to blow up our plane. Especially since it'll take us another twenty-four hours to repair that right wing so we can go home."

Athena rocks on her heels. Key fob still up. "Fuck's this shit about your nerds playing with me and the dog and the pregnant girl then?"

Oliver shrugs. "Whether you like it or not, if what you say is true, then you're the last vestiges of Frankie's technology." He locks eyes with Athena. "You're it."

Athena sneers.

Can't think of anything worse.

She and Michelle and Dogmeat are the last parts of Frankie left.

Athena says, "You'll get us to California?"

Oliver nods. "You'll protect us with the same loyalty as an NCR trooper?"

Athena checks the mag on her 1911. "Feed me some ammo."

5.

Athena waits till everyone calms the hell down. Herself included.

Her arrival apparently being such an earth-shattering event.

Never imagined she meant much to anyone other than David.

But now she's got a few badges.

Savior.

Badass fighter.

Lunatic.

. . . Drunk.

. . . Asshole.

. . . Murderer.

. . . Remnant of Frankie.

Athena pops the Hellcat trunk. Rubs her face.

Dogmeat stands next to her in the C-130 cargo bay. His tail ready to wag madly at a moment's notice.

Athena says to him, "You just ate."

He sits. Whines. Lifts his right paw and taps it against Athena's thigh.

"All right, fine." She grabs a can of beef stew. "But only cuz I assume you were starving your ass off a few days ago." Opens the can and sets it on the ground.

Dogmeat gobbles the food up as fast as he can. Trots outside to relieve himself. The troopers give him his space. Then offer their palms and hands to his nose. The canine's presence adds some familiarity and levity to their seemingly forever-fucked situation.

One guy in particular starts to scratch him behind the ears. The pooch responds by leaning against the trooper and rubbing his snout against the guy's uniform.

The guy pets and pats. Till he feels the dog's rear metal leg.

Realization dawns on the guy's face. He jerks back. Almost falls over his own feet. Raises his rifle. Points it at Dogmeat.

Dogmeat's ears shoot up. He pins em back against his head. Snarls.

Athena growls. Shouts. "*Hey.*" Pistol already in her hand. She targets the trooper spooked by Dogmeat's chrome. "You hurt that dog I'll goddamn feed you to him."

The guy scrunches his face at Athena. At the other troopers. "You insane, woman? It could be one of those *things* Frankie made."

Athena's aim doesn't waver. "He ain't."

Which she doesn't actually know for sure. But if anyone's gonna take Dogmeat out, it's gonna be her.

Principle of the thing and all.

Oliver steps out into the open from behind some engineers and technicians working on the C-130's damaged wing. He barks at the spooked trooper. "Carlos, leave it alone. We've already had one Mexican standoff today. That's enough."

Athena wonders in that instant if Oliver just made a goofy racist joke or not, but she keeps her mouth shut. Stares down Carlos. Gun still in hand.

Carlos relents. Lowers his rifle. Slings it.

He and Dogmeat stare at one another for a moment. Two. Finally Carlos reaches out and offers his hand again for the dog to sniff.

Dogmeat offers the soldier a short, deep bark. Turns tail. Trots away.

Athena chuckles. Smirks at Oliver with a shrug in her shoulders.

Oliver doesn't seem to think it's quite as funny as she does. His face remains blank and unsmiling. He says, "The pregnant girl was asking after you. I can take you to her if you want."

Athena holsters her 1911. "You hide the chick in some air duct somewhere or something?" She figures it can't be too hard to find Michelle in a single airplane.

"Has more to do with the fact that my guards will shoot you if I'm not around."

"Ah." Athena nods at the ground. "Fair."

Oliver makes his way up the ramp. He brushes by Athena. Steps around the Hellcat. Marches toward the hood. The dividing wall in front of the Dodge.

He grabs the latch on a door Athena didn't even notice. Says, "Everything behind this door is mine and the NCR's. You wanna be weird about the car and the dog and the girl? Fine. But remember what I said."

Athena cocks an eyebrow at the Republic sergeant. Gestures for him to get on with it.

He shoulders the door open. Nods to someone Athena can't see. Continues in.

Athena steps through the doorway after him. Eyeballs the four guards standing with guns in-hand just on the other side. More guys and gals with M4s. Military surplus uniforms.

They protect the rest of the aircraft and its precious cargo.

Dozens of crates of ammunition and weapons. Enough MREs to feed a small army for a year. Water. Technology that— even if it ain't up to snuff compared to Frankie's stuff—is at least modern and well cared-for.

There are rows of bunkbeds. Beyond that, an infirmary area. Unmoving bodies racked three high on cots that flip out from the walls. Intravenous drips implanted in wounded trooper's arms.

Athena looks around. Impressed enough.

Oliver keeps walking. NCR soldiers salute as he passes. He stops. Tugs at a curtain in the infirmary.

Michelle's there on a bed. Buried under blankets. IV attached to her arm. Heart and other health monitors lead away to machines Athena can scarcely believe exist anymore, let alone fuckin function.

The pregnant brunette smirks when she sees the Hellcat driver. Winces when that meager movement pulls at the bandage on her neck.

Athena smirks back. "They taking good care of you?"

Michelle nods. Says, "Can't complain." Her voice a scratchy whisper. Cracked. "Hot food and nice painkillers."

Athena chances a glance at Oliver.

The sergeant keeps his eyes on the pregnant woman.

Athena says to Michelle: "What'd you wanna talk to me about? Ollie here—"

Oliver's gaze snaps to Athena. He grimaces.

Athena corrects herself. "*Oliver* here said you were asking for me."

Michelle grunts. Tries to nod. She winces again. Lifts a hand to her throat.

Athena looks at Oliver. "You mind?"

The NCR sergeant's eyes bounce from Athena to Michelle and back.

He seems to need to mull it over in his brain, but Athena doesn't have a clue why.

Finally, he nods. Says, "Other side of the infirmary here, you're gonna see a short set of stairs leading up. That's the command deck. Meet me there." He looks to Michelle. "Ma'am." Then he ambles off.

Athena shuts the curtain to Michelle's little area. Leans in over the pregnant woman. "Is this the part where we agree we need to get the fuck away from these people?"

Michelle shakes her head. "Jesus, no." She rubs her pregnant belly. "Very much the opposite of that. I think the New California Republic are the best chance my baby's gonna have."

Athena grumbles. "This shit never pans out."

"Look—" Michelle grunts. Adjusts herself on her bed. "Look, yeah, I know. They're kinda uptight and stuff but. . .these people are part of a *real* military. Not some creepy raider cult or a militia. I can forgive the 'honor and service' dogma provided they're not into raping and eating human flesh." The pregnant chick pans her eyes around the C-130. "They have a working *plane*. When was the last time you saw a working plane?"

"It ain't working right now."

Michelle sighs. "You know what I mean."

Athena grunts. Stands with her hands on her hips. "I know they're curious about us cuz of what we went through with Frankie."

"What do you mean?"

"My leg. Dogmeat's leg. You and your baby. The New California Republic—or at least Oliver—thinks we might be the keys to recovering Frankie's tech."

Michelle squints at Athena. "I'm gonna assume you didn't fully explain *why* none of Frankie's tech exists anymore."

Athena shrugs.

Michelle says, "Well, I don't think that's what they're doing to my baby. Oliver and the doctors here already checked on him. He's gonna be a healthy baby boy."

Him.

Dawns on Athena she's never once bothered to ask anything about the little human growing inside Michelle. Never cared to. She was always too distracted by trying to stay alive.

And drinking.

Smoking.

Driving.

Athena sniffs. *Whatever.* She says, "How you know they won't just yank that little rugrat outta you and play science with it?"

"They gave me their word. I can finally say I have a future. They need young mothers and healthy babies for the New Eden project in the redwoods."

Athena's lips become a tight line. Almost bloodless. "Do they."

* * *

Athena stomps up the stairs. Passes under a bulkhead. Enters the command deck.

It's a small room next to the cockpit. One with a table scattered with diagrams. Drawings. Computer screens nearby flash maps. Parts of messages. Flight patterns. There's radio equipment. Five chairs wait in various places.

An operations manual on the wall clarifies that this ain't just a big C-130 Hercules.

It's a massive sonuvabitch C-130J *Super* Hercules.

Oliver sits in one of the chairs. A folder in his lap.

Athena says, "What'd you need."

He points to the random assortment of chairs. "Have a seat if you want."

Athena doesn't, but she plops her ass down anyway. Pops a cigarette between her lips.

Oliver eyes her. "Close the door if you're gonna smoke. Rather not have that shit filtering down into the infirmary."

Athena does. Reseats herself. Lights up. "Why am I here, Oliver?" She finds a disposable coffee cup that's only got a thin film of dark brown at the bottom. Uses it as an ashtray.

"Figure if I'm gonna suggest the NCR should be allowed to prod your chrome leg, then I should be a little more forthcoming with regards to the situation."

"You mean the fuckfest here, or—"

"I mean the whole situation. The New California Republic's situation." He stands. Drops the folder into his chair. Takes a deep breath. "Can I bum one?"

Athena tilts her head. Shrugs. Digs a stogie from her pack and rolls it across the table toward Oliver. Then slides her lighter to him.

Oliver sparks his cigarette. Tosses the lighter back. He takes a lungful. Blows smoke. Looks at the burning cig. Watches the blue-grey wisps curl around his fingers. Says, "Just a stress thing, y'know." He taps the table. Uncurls a worn map of the western United States.

Athena notices that there are cities with markings on em. Some circled in red or black. Others have blue squares. More are simply crossed out.

A *lot* more.

San Diego is gone. The entire Baja peninsula is scratched out. Phoenix and Tucson have big X's on em. Goodbye Las Vegas. Los Angeles. San Jose. Sacramento. And effectively every town in the American southwest.

What the NCR has—Athena assumes the circles means they're under NCR control—is Salt Lake City. Reno. Sierra Army Depot. Beale Air Force Base. The Redwood National Forest. Eugene. Seattle.

Athena doesn't know if this is good progress or not. The NCR obviously has considerable manpower and materials, but they haven't managed to take hold of much in the decade and a half since the bug hit.

On the other hand, organizing a trained army takes a fuckin while.

Athena ashes her cigarette. "What am I supposed to do with this?"

"Just trying to impress upon you the uphill battle we face."

"Considering the nightmarish shit I've seen, that's not really necessary."

"Maybe not." Oliver ashes his cigarette. "But if you can at least see the progress we've made, it might help persuade you to let us look over that robotic leg of yours."

"Losing my leg once has made me kinda attached to it, is the thing."

Oliver rubs his face. Scratches his neck. Puffs on his cigarette. He groans.

Athena shakes her head. "I mean, what's the point? We're just walking dead."

"Not all of us. That's what the New Eden project is for. We're trying to *rebuild*, is the point. We have a good foothold across the west. If NCR technicians could reverse-engineer whatever your leg is made out of—how it works—we could improve our armor. Our weaponry. Instead of the Iron Cross overwhelming and murdering half my platoon, just one Republic trooper could withstand a raider assault solo."

"And I should help cuz you're the good guys, right?"

"*Yes.*"

Athena grunts. "I'm fuzzy on the whole good-bad thing. Far as I can tell, it's open season. Different groups have different goals. And you're all assholes."

Oliver stares at the Hellcat driver. Keeps smoking. He grabs the folder on his chair. Flips it open. Tosses it down in front of Athena. "I guarantee you, we're not the worst thing out here."

Athena plucks the folder up. Sees an official-looking stamp at the top that reads "NCR Official Use Only."

It's a dossier.

The first page is a blank sheet that warns the contents are classified. Blah blah blah. The second page has a photo in the upper right corner. Some insane bald bastard rocking S&M gear.

A chain that links his pierced nipples through holes cut into a black leather vest. Black chaps with the freak's studded banana hammock exposed.

Athena arches her eyebrows. Mutters. "Looks like some sex show reject."

Oliver's silent.

She keeps reading.

NAME: UNKNOWN

ALIAS: WESTERN DEVIL

ALLEGIANCE: IRON CROSS

ACTIVE: YES

HIGH VALUE TARGET. ELIMINATE. DO NOT ATTEMPT CAPTURE.

Athena sniffs. "Well. I've heard the name before. Still don't know what this has to do with me. Seems like you've got your work cut out for you, though. I mean, if you're sticking to this saving the world gig."

Oliver takes a final drag from his cigarette. Drops it into a coffee cup. The stogie hisses. "The Western Devil? He's the leader of the Iron Cross."

Athena sucks her teeth. "Okay." She thinks about Bullhorn, back at Frankie's. The raider talking about how even he had a boss. "Still don't—"

"You know what the problem with making a name for yourself is, *Hellcat*? Becoming a sorta living legend that people *talk* about? You make yourself a target. And the Western Devil wants you real, real bad." He waits a beat. Eyeballs her.

Red lights flash to life inside the plane. An emergency siren sounds.

Athena's hand unconsciously falls to her 1911. She smells a backstabbing.

Oliver sees the movement. Stares her down. "Don't."

"Why not? Better to go out guns blazing."

"Yeah, except the NCR wants you as bad as the Iron Cross."

Athena stands. Drops her cigarette. "Nice to be needed, huh?"

6.

Athena jogs down through the C-130. The yanks a scoped rifle and some ammo from one of the racks on the wall. An M39 EMR chambered in 7.62mm. Plus two spare mags.

She runs by Michelle. The pregnant girl's face is scrunched. Like she's confused.

Athena shakes her head at the brunette. Keeps jogging. Pauses at the C-130's ramp. Peeks around the corner.

There's another Iron Cross asshole down at the far end of the tarmac again. That spot to the south where the solo surviving cocksucker bailed onto I-70 last time. Now he's flanked by two more trucks. Big ones. Garbage trucks that've been refitted to carry boarding parties but with spikes on their sides to dissuade anyone from doing the same.

And they're just. . .sitting there. Waiting.

Athena looks back into the plane. Locks eyes with Oliver as he marches toward her. She holds up three fingers and points downrange.

Oliver nods. The Republic sergeant points to an access ladder embedded in the wall that'll let her get on top of the C-130J.

Athena curls away from the ramp. Huffs her way up the ladder. Pops the hatch there. Crawls onto the fuselage. She stays on her belly. Peers through the rifle's optics.

She can see the bastard Iron Cross goons a helluva lot better. The one at the center, flanked by those garbage trucks, he stands in the bed of a Ford F250. Bullhorn in hand.

The bullhorn goon gesticulates wildly. White flags are raised on each vehicle. Waved by crazy-eyed raiders. Bright sheets that flutter among the skulls and ramshackle machinery.

Athena keeps her crosshairs on the bullhorn goon. Tracks him as the Iron Cross vehicles push up toward the stationary NCR plane.

They come to a stop about a hundred meters away.

The goon shouts into his mechanical mouthpiece. "All right, all right. Everyone relax. No shooting. White flags, see?" The goon gestures.

Athena can't see Oliver, but she can hear him say, "I'm not agreeing to anything. Scum like you have no honor. Speak your piece. You've got thirty seconds."

"Oof." The goon feigns being hit. "You wound me, sir." He sighs. "But, so be it. I've talked it over with the big man himself and—" the goon holds up a finger "—if you hand over the Hellbitch, we'll let you and your NCR pukes fly, fly away. Hell, we'll even leave your strongholds alone for a month. How can you beat a deal like that?"

Oliver doesn't hesitate. "We don't make deals with raiders. Get fucked. I highly recommend you leave. *Now.*"

"You're making a real nasty mistake. Not just for yourselves here, but for all the NCR people. How much spilled blood is the Hellbitch worth to you assholes? Do you think the Western Devil is going to *stop* because you said '*no?*'"

"Time's up."

"I'm warn—"

Athena pulls the trigger. Sends a powerful 7.62 round through the bullhorn goon's throat. Snaps her aim down. Splatters the face of the Ford F250 driver.

She doesn't think she can punch through the armor plating over the front of the garbage trucks.

Not that it matters.

Both explode in a hail of fiery wreckage. Burning Iron Cross corpses flop out like ragdolls set aflame.

Athena grunts. Slides down the ladder into the body of the plane. She catches a glimpse of Oliver and a young female trooper in his command dropping their spent rocket launcher tubes.

She shouts to Oliver: "How long we got?"

Oliver puts his hands out. Puffs his cheeks. "Was about six hours between you kicking their ass last time and us kicking their ass this time." He snaps his fingers at an unknown male soldier. Young. "How fast can you and Kelly get us flying?"

The young trooper groans. Scratches the side of his head. "Fuck me, I. . .We got the other two damaged engines up to speed. So we'll shoot for those six hours, Sarge."

"Don't shoot f—"

"Just get it done, I know. *I know.*"

"Good man. Make it happen." Oliver licks his lips. Says to Athena, "It's gonna be close."

"It's gonna be bad."

"That too."

"But as long as you've got explosives, we should be fine. Just fry the fuckers." Athena leans against her Hellcat in the cargo bay.

"Sure." Oliver kicks the two spent M72 LAWs at his feet. "Except these were the last we had, if I'm not mistaken."

Athena lights a cigarette. Pops the Hellcat trunk. Lays the M39 rifle inside. The two mags. Not cuz she's thinking of stealing em. Cuz she needs to free her arms to haul out a spare gas can.

She plops it on the floor of the cargo bay with a *clang*. "Mountains keep em from hitting us from the north or the east. That leaves the south and the west. And we've seen they keep poking around from the south." Athena breathes smoke. "I say we give em a little minefield to drive through on the southern tarmac. I-70 too."

Oliver winces at the thought. "Roadside bombs. IEDs."

"If some terrorist fuckboys could figure it out, I'm sure we can too." Athena walks down into the dirt. Points. "In between the buildings and the hill there for starters. It'll be dark when the shitbirds come back. They won't be able to see the bombs. But we'll see the booms." She makes a fist. Puffs her cheeks. Expands her fingers away from her palm. "Boom."

Oliver holds up a hand. "Lotta my soldiers here, they ain't gonna like the idea of planting roadside bombs—for obvious reasons. I'll make sure one of my people helps make the damned things, but you're gonna have to place em yourself."

Athena pulls a face like she's gonna sneeze. "This is about survival, you dipshit." A quick sneer that fades away. "But you guys are holding fast and steady to this honor thing, huh?"

"It's what separates the NCR from murderous scum."

Athena grunts. Smokes. "Right. Of course."

* * *

The NCR kid's name is Sammy. Quiet and annoyed-looking at all times. What the twenty-something guy probably mistakes for stoicism.

Athena doesn't bother making small talk. Or any talk.

She's pretty sure the troopers are humorless, anyway. At least right now, in this situation. Only exception might be Oliver, but even he's kinda stuffy.

An unlit cigarette bounces on her lips while she works. Threads cabling through the bombs she's making so when a raider or a wheel tugs the wire, kaboom.

Sammy packs a bundle of .50-caliber shells around a gunpowder charge. Looks over at the Hellcat driver as she does the same.

They've made ten.

And twelve should do it.

Six spaced along the tarmac. Three along I-70. Three for the road into the airport.

Sammy says, "Think this is gonna work?"

"I think it'd be a great idea for your mechanics to get that engine working again."

* * *

Sammy helps Athena carefully—oh so fuckin carefully—load the IEDs into the Hellcat.

She lights her long-awaited cigarette. Then has to jump in front of Dogmeat to prevent the pooch from throwing himself in the back and blowing em all to hell.

She shakes her head. "Please don't." Leads the canine around to the passenger side.

He takes Michelle's place at shogun.

Athena rolls the Hellcat down the C-130J ramp backward. Offers a curt wave to Oliver. Sets out south along the tarmac.

The raider wrecks and corpses here are still warm and they still stink. A noxious mix of burning rubber and fuel and flesh and hair.

She tries to ignore the stench. Finds a flat area of landing strip that the raiders are likely to use. Drive their obscene trucks through. She grabs an IED from the backseat. Some like fat thermoses built into used artillery shells. Others the size of lunchboxes.

Athena tucks one in the husk of a truck's wheel well. The business end tilted up at an angle so it'll explode low and hard against the underside of anyone driving by. She runs the tripwire out about ten feet. Uses a heavy club hammer to pound a short spike into a crack in the asphalt. Wraps the tripwire around the spike till it's taught and a couple feet off the ground.

The sun starts its downward descent near the horizon. Light morphs from its usual sickly pale yellow to orange. Shadows of the dead and their machines grow long.

Athena looks toward the NCR troopers and their plane. The small figures scuttling around. Trying to unfuck their engine.

She doesn't hate em for focusing on saving their asses.

She *does* kinda hate em for sticking her with the task of setting up booby traps while they can console themselves that they play "fair." Or whatever the fuck the mentality is.

Why handicap yourself in this doomed world with the burden of honor?

Her brain chirps: *Well, when you don't, you end up with the Iron Cross. Or any number of vile assholes who'll kill, rape, and eat you. Not necessarily in that order.*

Yeah.

Western Devil looks like a good candidate for that.

Athena finishes placing her traps. Hops back into the Hellcat. Drives out beyond the southern airstrip. Into the dirt and dust between the tarmac and I-70. She locates breaks in the airport fence. Plants an IED. Walks to where the guardrail's split. Plants an IED.

She drives down I-70 a stretch. Retraces her path toward the airport entrance. Gets on Horizon Drive. There's a Chevron gas station that could use an IED—so she threads a tripwire from the street to the pumps.

Athena plants the final three bombs liberally along the path to the airport.

Then she returns to the C-130J. Parks again in the metal beast's belly.

Athena stays in the driver's seat. Digs into the MRE Oliver gave her. Separates everything that ain't a real meal from the main pouch. Uses some bottled water to activate the chemical heater.

Dogmeat sniffs at it and whines.

The Hellcat driver shakes her head. "No fuckin way."

Dogmeat whines one more time before he squirms between the front seats to curl up in the back.

Athena sips whiskey and smokes and downs a painkiller while the grub cooks. Feels like she's done enough for the day to help the NCR and doesn't offer any more.

Republic troopers stay busy in the rearview. They move supplies from the field into the plane. Sandbags they don't bother with. Turrets and mounted guns they do. Soldiers bolt twin .50-caliber Browning machine guns to each side of the loading ramp.

A thought occurs to Athena as she spoons *fettuccine Alfredo* down her gullet: *Are they planning to fly this thing with the ramp open?*

Turn it into a gunship or somesuch.

Great fuckin idea. Provided the Dodge is secured and doesn't go careening out the back.

Athena steps out to locate a soldier who can tie down the Hellcat. If she loses the car at this point, she'll lose her fuckin mind. She makes sure her door's shut, knowing how fidgety Dogmeat can be. The pooch seems to ache for a fight.

Blue-green lights snap on overhead to illuminate the cargo bay. They're so bright it's like being in Times Square.

She's still holding the hot bag of noodles when she barks at a young trooper to make sure the Hellcat won't budge. "That vehicle is the most important thing in the world to me."

The Republic grunt nods. Can't find a reason to disagree.

An explosion thunders through the evening air. Somewhere in the direction of I-70. Not close enough to be on the airstrip though.

Black smoke curls up into the sky from the interstate. Near the break in the guardrail.

Iron Cross are early.

Athena drops her grub. Runs to the Hellcat trunk. Grabs the M39. Climbs up to the roof of the plane. The fuselage under her shudders as the C-130 pilot turns the engines over.

But she sees the bastards through the scope. A dozen vehicles of varying sizes—Fords and Chevys and garbage trucks and even a damn bus—kick up dust on their trek to the front of the airport.

Another dozen veer off and form a wide line to the south. In the fading light, their headlights are bright, angry eyes.

Makes Athena think of riot police during protests. Where they form a wall and crush anyone unlucky enough to be in front of em.

Also makes her think: *Ah, fuck.*

7.

If the Western Devil's here, he ain't showing himself.

Athena imagines the weird fucker is gonna have some outlandish kinda vehicle all to himself. She doesn't see anything that fits the bill. Not yet. It's all repurposed and scavenged raider shit. Nothing extravagant enough for the leathered up weirdo and his chained together nipples and his studded banana hammock.

Oliver shouts up from inside the cargo bay. "Watch yourself when we start taxiing. You fall and it's probably lights out."

Athena shouts back: "You secure my goddamn car?"

"Hang on." Pause. "Yeah. You want that dog in the back?"

"Better than him running out and getting his ass killed."

Considering what Dogmeat's been through, he might actually be safer *away* from humans. Seems he can take care of himself. She doesn't point this out.

It goes calm and still except for the fat plane's engines spooling up.

Athena has no doubt that Oliver's troops are doing what they need to. Getting into defensive positions. Tidying up their shit. Watching the enemy.

But she can't hear a damn thing over the roar of the four turboprops.

She keeps her aim as steady as she can. Butt of the EMR buttressed against her shoulder. Barrel of the rifle resting on her outstretched forearm. The leather-clad Hellcat driver a literal pinup atop the cargo hauling C-130J.

The scope—a Schmidt Bender PMII—gives her eyes on anything inside 2,000 meters. So of course these fuckers sit just outside that range. Still on I-70. Their vehicles wait. Unmoving.

Athena peels her eyes away from the rifle optics. Pans her gaze to the right so she can follow the other group of raiders. The psychos on their way to the front gate. They should be getting near the Chevron bomb she rigged to blow. . .any. . .second. . . .

Now.

She sees the flash and the fireball a second before she hears the titanic, gut-rumbling explosion from the Chevron station. With any luck, most of the Iron Cross heading that way are crispy critters.

The Iron Cross to the south whip their arms around. These smudges in the scope. Illuminated by the running lights and headlights of their mad assault vehicles.

Seems like they're kinda pissed about that gas station explosion.

Two more explosions rock the air. Both from the southern line of raider shitheads. Twin flashes and smoke clouds and destroy two Iron Cross vehicles as they leave I-70 and enter the airport grounds.

Athena grins.

Ten remain. They barrel toward the NCR aircraft. Their fuzziness snaps into clarity once they pass the two thousand meter threshold.

For shits and giggles, Athena tries to line up a shot. Aims for where she thinks one of the truck's front windows is gonna be. She holds her breath. Fires off a round.

And. . . .

Nothing.

She wants to try for another shot, but she'd rather save the ammo.

Iron Cross trucks gain speed when they hit the tarmac. The intensity of their attack feels a helluva lot more earnest. The sounds of their engines fight to be heard over the growing roar of the C-130J's turboprops.

Gunfire erupts from both the Iron Cross goons and the NCR troopers once the distance between em shrinks to a thousand meters. Great bursts of heavy weapons and small arms fire. Tracers streak through the air. Lasers that bounce from one side to the other.

Athena keeps her finger off the trigger. Waits and watches as the raider scum approach the field of wrecks and IEDs. . . .

It's glorious.

A symphony of thunder and lighting. Screams and gunfire. Tracers zoom through the night sky in seeming slow motion as flames bloom under enemy trucks and send em flying. Careening. End over end and into one another.

Five bombs touch off. Five trucks rupture.

Iron Cross goons stumble in confusion. Some ejected from their vehicles. Others wounded in collisions. They hold their sides. Their arms. Some totter on weak legs and try merely to *find* their arms.

These dirtbags...These dirtbags Athena enjoys taking out. A bullet for every shellshocked raider. She aims for heads and necks. Silhouettes that spray bodily fluids in front of the pyres of their asshole pals.

Ain't all of em though. Five raider assault vehicles are still inbound.

Athena takes a knee. Drops the empty mag from her rifle. Slams a fresh one home. Gets back to causing damage.

She doesn't aim as careful now. She wants to pound their windshields with 7.62 rounds. She growls. Focuses on pulling the trigger. Focuses on a volume of fire that cracks the glass of the Ford and Chevy pickups.

Mounted guns manned by NCR troopers below do the rest. They tear through the metal and kill engine blocks. Make the trucks useless. Make the occupants bloody, hole-filled ruinations of flesh.

Athena creeps along the fuselage. The plane's lights blink around her. She lowers her rifle and tries to find fresh targets. Comes up empty.

She and the C-130J are surrounded by death.

The Hellcat driver shrugs. "Not half bad." And almost loses her footing as the aircraft below her starts to taxi. It hooks around to face west.

Athena climbs inside. Secures the roof access hatch. She nods to the two gunners that stand on the ramp. Both watch her with something akin to appreciation before they return their attention to the .50-cals.

The airstrip behind the C-130J is illuminated by the green-blue glow of the plane's cargo bay lights. They pass over the cracked tarmac at a snail's pace. Newly-repaired engines on the wings roar with fresh ferocity. The asphalt underneath becomes a blur.

An airhorn blares from the right of the ramp.

Headlights split the darkness.

The Iron Cross bus screams onto the airstrip. Chains and a boarding party of lunatic goons dangle along its sides. Both the vehicle and its psychotic passengers look singed. Probably from the Chevron blast.

May have taken them a while to get themselves together, but they're keeping pace with the C-130J now. And gaining.

The bus driver leans out his window. Points a blackened finger at Athena. He screams and laughs. Eyes wild. "We're coming for you Hellbitch. We don't forgive. We don't *forget*." He reaches inside. Grabs something square. "You can't hide from the Western Devil."

He holds the box outside by its handle.

It's clear.

There's a head inside.

Athena recognizes it as Bullhorn's.

Thinks: *Shit. I only killed. . .like. . .a couple dozen of em. Dunno why they're so pissed.*

She sneers. Growls. Pulls her 1911. Sends a .45 round into the driver's arm, right at the wrist. The bones shatter. Snap through the skin. Sudden white protrusions that flay the tissue.

The .50-cal gunners open up on the bus. Big fat Browning machine gun bullets turn the bodies of the raiders that hang on the bus's side into chunky meat. Entire appendages explode.

Arms and legs and skulls. Torsos erupt in volcanoes of blood that rain down the sides of the Iron Cross vehicle.

Athena keeps her eyes locked on the driver's while the NCR troopers brutalize his bus. She walks backward to the Hellcat. Pops the trunk. Grabs some whiskey. Takes a pull. Lights a cigarette. Slams the trunk and rests her ass right against the bumper.

She gives the driver the middle finger a moment before his face is torn apart by heavy weapons fire.

Smoke billows from the front of the bus.

The bloodied vehicle slows. Catches fire.

The C-130J tilts its nose up.

Athena wraps her left hand around a tie-down keeping the Hellcat secure. Her right keeps the precious whiskey safe. The cigarette dangles from her lips.

The ground seems to fall away from the cargo plane.

Just perpetual darkness with hints of light across distances she can't guess at.

Athena wonders if this is what it's like to travel through space.

She holds onto the whiskey with her pinky, ring finger, and thumb. Plucks the stogie free with her index and middle finger. She regards the booze and the cancer stick.

Thinks: *Probably not, but it should be.*

Athena checks the backseat of the Hellcat. Notices that poor Dogmeat is being smooshed against the headrests and the rear window by gravity and inertia.

His eyes are huge. Panicked. It's easy to see that he's wildly confused and *certain* that this shit shouldn't be happening.

She pouts. Makes a mental note to give the pooch some decent grub.

Then catches herself.

Athena's getting cozy. Cute. Friendly. Getting friendly means letting your guard down. Which is what makes people dead.

She sniffs. Smokes. Drinks. Repeats her mantra in her head: *I am strong. I am death. I am the absence of forgiveness. There is no poetry for me, for I am that. Strength. Death. The absence of forgiveness.*

Athena blinks at the darkness outside. Does the same to the floor of the plane. Cracks her neck. Smokes a little more. Drinks a little more.

Figures: *Fuck it.*

She's gonna give Dogmeat some decent food.

The plane levels off. The ramp closes.

Athena walks to the machine gunners. Offers the two—a woman and a man just a hair younger than her—whiskey from the bottle she's been working on.

Nobody says much. They just hold each other's eyes. Chuckle. Suck booze. Hold the amber liquid up between gulps and toast one another without words.

Slaughter like that brings folks together.

All the gore and terror.

Oliver's voice sounds over the aircraft's comm system. "This is your captain speaking. I wanna congratulate my troopers here for a major victory over the scum of the Iron Cross. It shows those bastards what I already know: the NCR will *not* bow down. We will *not* submit to their madness. We *will* persevere in our crusade to reclaim the wastes."

Athena's eyes bounce between the gunners. Both look proud. Stoic. Their chins held high. Chests puffed.

The overall mood throughout the plane seems to be the same. There are no cheers. Many, many stern faces, though.

Oliver continues: "And I want to thank Athena for her assistance—the woman I think most of you know as the Hellcat. She's already proven herself invaluable. From this point forward, I want all of you, and the New California Republic, to consider her a sister in arms." He pauses. "We're making a straight run to Salt Lake City for refuel and resupply. After that, Reno. Get some shuteye if you can, troopers. We land in about an hour. Hellcat, please join me in the cockpit."

Athena winces. Already feels like she's the focus of too much attention.

She'd rather not be singled out. But here she is.

Mahalo.

The two gunners take another turn with the whiskey bottle. Each raises their drink to her as they gulp alcohol.

Athena snuffs out her cigarette. Stops by the Dodge on her way through the plane. Opens the door and gives Dogmeat a scratch behind the ears to reassure him.

She stops at the big separation door. Isn't sure if she should knock or shoulder it open the same way Oliver did. Decides to knock.

An NCR trooper on the other side waves Athena through.

She struts through storage. The infirmary. Sees Michelle is sleeping and leaves the pregnant chick alone.

Heads up to the command deck. Knocks on the forward door there, too.

A young soldier with a monstrous scar across his cheek greets her. Nods. Stands back so she can enter.

The cockpit is bigger than she anticipated. Wide with four chairs and a semicircle of window panes that provide a panoramic view for the pilots.

Granted, to the naked eye, it's a panorama of blackness.

That's what the screens and readouts and dials and switches are for. All of which she finds panic-inducing and understands in only a distant way. She's glad she doesn't have to deal with any of it.

Oliver looks over his shoulder at Athena. He taps the older woman in the seat next to his own. She gives Athena a glance, then nods to her boss.

The NCR sergeant removes his headset. Stands. Gestures for the Hellcat driver to follow him.

They end up back on the command deck.

Oliver takes the same ratty seat he had before. Leans back. Stares at the ceiling.

Athena takes her pack of cigarettes out. Tosses it and a lighter onto the table.

Oliver reaches for it. Says, "Thanks." Sparks a stogie.

Before Athena can ask what the hell is going on, another man joins em.

Oliver waves smoke from his eyes. Points to the new arrival. "Corporal Ben Whitmore, meet Athena Kozielewski. The Hellcat."

Ben regards Athena. Says, "Ma'am."

Athena shakes her head. "Definitely not a ma'am."

Ben arches his eyebrows. Sits. Like the other troopers, he's fit. Strong. A little on the younger side, but born well before the germ hit.

Oliver says, "Ben's my second in command. He's the man to talk to about gear and repairs and whatever you need once we resupply in Salt Lake City."

Athena nods half-heartedly. Crosses her arms over her chest. "Okay."

"I'm considering you an advisor. That's why you're here." Oliver ashes his cigarette. Looks to Ben. "Where do we stand?"

Ben cocks an eye at Athena. Grimaces. Seems like the guy ain't used to talking in front of anyone who isn't really part of the Republic.

He takes a breath.

Says, "We lost half our platoon. Supplies are gone. We're fucked as a fighting unit and damn lucky to be alive." Ben tilts his head toward Athena. "I assume the stories about her are true. Otherwise we wouldn't bother."

Oliver says, "We wouldn't."

Athena rolls her eyes. Reaches for the cigarettes on the table. Grabs one. Lights one. "Fuck is the issue?"

"Well. . . ." Ben eyeballs Oliver. Tries to gauge his commanding officer. "Up till this point, we skirmished with the Iron Cross. Let em take towns we didn't need."

"But."

"*But.*" Ben looks to Oliver again.

Oliver nods. "Yeah. I think we've started a war."

8.

Athena allows herself a dumb joke.

Aww. You declared war on account of little old me? P'shaw!

The wretchedness of it has a rhythm, though.

And she has to think for a few minutes about *how many* assholes she's killed.

A lot.

Iron Cross. Frankie's freaks. Wraiths and Trakers.

A hundred? More.

She doesn't feel bad about a single one.

So with that kinda death toll, ain't a shock she's wanted. NCR is interested in her leg for the technology. Iron Cross wants to put her in chains and or rape and or eat her to make a point about people fuckin with em. Trakers probably want the same.

Makes her long for the anonymous chaos of the east coast.

Athena watches out the cargo plane's cockpit windows as they come in low over Salt Lake City International airport. It's all lit up. A bright expanse of asphalt and machinery in the darkness.

Looks like they've set up the terminals as a forward operating base.

She sees patrols of trucks. Offroads with machine guns mounted in the beds. A few military vehicles as well. Armored personnel carriers. More planes. Even a couple of helicopters that hover near the outskirts of the airport. Their spotlights punch through the night air. Scan for raiders and other nightmares of the wastes.

Oliver talks to someone on the ground through his headset. "We're coming in on the eastern side and we'll taxi over toward terminal one." She looks over his shoulder at Athena. "Yessir. She's with us."

Athena cocks an eye. The C-130J begins its descent. She reaches out to steady herself against the wall of the cabin.

The big craft's wheels squeal when they touch down. The whole plane bounces once. Then settles into a rumbling roll.

Oliver punches buttons and flips switches.

Athena can hear the whine of the engines die down.

An NCR soldier uses two flashlights with glowing orange cones on the end to guide the plane into position. It doesn't dock—there's no extended walkway to latch onto the aircraft the way you'd see on an old commercial jet—it simply comes to a stop. More NCR soldiers march out to greet it.

Athena follows Oliver through the plane. He barks orders at his subordinates. Tells em to get the wounded into the terminal. Tells em to make sure the plane is refueled. Explosives and medical supplies restocked.

He hits a button on the cargo bay wall. The ramp opens. A big metal tongue that dips to the tarmac.

Oliver says to Athena, "Gonna need you to move the car so we have a clear path for resupply. Park where you want. Nobody's gonna touch it."

Athena dips her head so she can see onto the asphalt.

There are three stuffy-looking NCR troops standing shoulder-to-shoulder. Probably officers. Their faces are dour. The center sourpuss has an eagle insignia on his collar. Which makes him a colonel.

Dude definitely outranks Oliver.

She's not sure if that changes her situation.

The colonel locks eyes with her. His expression still as though he sucked on a lemon for dinner.

Oliver snaps to attention. Salutes. "Colonel Forrester."

Forrester nods. "Sergeant." Returns the salute. "I want a full debrief on the Grand Junction incident before you continue on to Beale to meet with the Founders. It's looking like you and the Hellcat—" Forrester's eyebrows bounce "—have sent the Iron Cross completely over the edge."

Oliver takes a deep breath. "Yessir." He tells Athena, "Talk to Ben. I'll be back."

Athena grunts. Unlocks her car. Pops a cigarette between her lips and starts the Dodge up. She watches Oliver plod down the ramp in the driver's side mirror. Breathes smoke. Wonders what kind of dumb shit can go wrong now.

She throws the Hellcat into reverse. Backs outta the C-130J. Dogmeat trots after her and the car. She parks off to the side of the terminal. Steps out. Scratches Dogmeat behind the ears and looks around to make sure she ain't smoking next to something hilariously flammable.

Ben saunters off the plane. The young corporal directs soldiers who move the wounded on stretchers. He confers with NCR troops from the airport. Points toward fuel trucks that idle nearby.

Then he makes his way toward her. "Ma'am."

For whatever reason, that sets Athena off. Sticks in her mind. "Quit it with the 'ma'am' shit." She scratches her nose. Juts her chin in the direction of the military vehicles. The machine gun emplacements. "You ever get attacked here?"

"By. . .what? Raiders or bugs?"

"By whatever."

Ben shrugs. "Our operating bases have been established long enough at this point that the local wildlife knows to stay away." He looks out toward the choppers that circle in the night sky. Their blades *whumpwhumpwhump*. "Gunships tend to snuff out anything hostile before it gets close. Spiders and ants can't really compete with the firepower on a Venom or a Pave Hawk, y'know?"

"Raiders, though."

"Raiders and Iron Cross want what we have, yeah. No denying that. But our defenses always beat back their attacks."

Athena shakes her head. "More illusions of safety." She coughs. "That could change if you're not careful." She grabs at her chest. Groans. "Man."

"Well. . .you're a smoker. That's what happens. No offense."

Athena wipes a hand across her lips. There's a little bit of blood. Just a touch. A smear. On her palm. "'No offense.' Respect your elders, shitfuck. . .What am I? Ten years older than you?"

"Maybe."

Athena grins. Blood in her teeth. "You're a puppy compared to me—maybe—and you're alive on account of you got an army of fuckboys behind you." She gives Ben an angry, ugly smile. "Know what I got?" She points to the bullet-ridden Hellcat. "I got a car." She sniffs. "I got a gun."

"I wasn't trying to piss you off."

"You did." Athena coughs and pets Dogmeat. "*People* do." She spits a load of blood and saliva onto the tarmac. "The propped up 'right thing' deal. The pompousness." Reaches into the Hellcat. Retries her whiskey. Sucks the bottle. "Y'know, you. . . ." Athena swallows. Frowns. Cuts herself off.

She says, "Doesn't matter. I didn't know I was signing up for a boss, but I was. That asshole with the eagle insignia. Guess he's a ballbuster."

Ben steps toward her. "The Republic—"

Athena palms the 1911 on her thigh. Shakes her head. "The Republic does dick. You guys are dragging your parasitic asses across the face of a dead world. Same as you did before." She doesn't pull her pistol. Just lets her hand rest there near it. "You think humanity wasn't due for a culling?"

Ben puts up his hands. "I *think* you're a stubborn bitch. I think you're set in your ways and you don't want to believe the Republic is doing the right thing." His eyes are mad. Eyebrows arched down.

Athena scratches her cheek. "Fair. . .Know what's fucked up?"

"Everything?" Ben crosses his arms. "That's why we're here. That's why we're trying to change all this. You can't possibly say you'd rather the Western Devil and the Iron Cross be in charge of the country instead of us."

Choppers continue to *whumpwhumpwhump* around their heads in the darkness.

Athena takes a pull from her cigarette. "Two sides of the same coin. The new bosses vying for control like the old bosses." Pops a painkiller.

David blinks in her mind. But the memory's getting dim.

She fights it.

He's been dead for years and you still do your mourning from the bottom of a whiskey bottle. Or from behind a gun.

Athena grunts. "No. You're right. I'm not the kind of lady who wants *obvious* leather-daddy rapists in charge." She smirks. "What I *want* is for you to repair my car and gimme all your high explosives.

"*That* is the kind of lady I am."

NCR troopers roll Michelle off the plane about forty feet away.

Athena furrows her brow. Voice harsh. "Fuck are they doing with her."

"There's better medical equipment inside. In spite of your angry bullshit, we generally try to keep civilians alive. Especially if their baby is cancer—and germ-free."

Athena grunts. "So what's the life expectancy for you grunts here on the west coast?"

"If there aren't bullets involved? Random. Some folks seem invulnerable—Sergeant Bradley was a *farmer*. Isolated. But there's no real rhyme or reason." He pauses. Considers his words. "You're from New York?"

Athena nods.

Ben nods back. "Then you've traveled far enough to know that nobody knows anything."

Athena frowns. Stares at the tarmac near her boots.

Her brain screams at her: *Frankie said he knew something. Frankie said he was working on a cure. Frankie had research.*

Frankie had answers.

And you blew it all up.

Ben clears his throat. "Look. Michelle is being taken in for more appropriate medical attention. If you want, I can have the mechanics look over the Hellcat, but if it's cosmetic shit, I'm not gonna ask em to waste time on it."

Athena looks at the Dodge. "Fair."

"Yeah. Explosives and gas we can get you, though." He gestures toward the terminal. "Now, if you'll follow me, Oliver asked me to show you to your room."

"You got a bar inside?"

"If you head west from terminal one, you'll find the NCR lounge, we—"

"Save it." Athena grabs a fresh whiskey bottle from the Hellcat. Locks the car. "Just realized I don't care and I'd rather be alone."

Ben purses his lips. Walks toward Salt Lake City's airport.

Athena follows. Snaps her fingers.

Dogmeat relieves himself then trots into line.

Ben turns. Sees the pooch. "Animals aren't allowed inside."

Athena keeps walking. "Yeah, they are." Pushes the double doors into the main building.

First thing that strikes her is how damn bright it is. She has to blink.

Second is how goddamn beige and yellow and brown it is.

Athena sneers.

Dogmeat waits at her side.

The NCR troopers inside stop and stare at her. Same as every place.

They whisper under their breath.

Shit. There's the Hellcat. That woman. That fiend. That bitch. She's a savior and a scourge. Hero and a drunk.

How much damage can she do to us before we set her loose on the other bad guys.

. . . And where'd she get the dog.

A low growl rumbles in the back of Dogmeat and Athena's throats.

Ben walks by em.

They follow.

All amid a combination of hesitant eyes and sneers. Some soldiers who seem thrilled at Athena's presence and others who want nothing to do with her.

They're all armed.

A hundred or more people who've been motivated to join the NCR's cause.

Athena and Dogmeat pass alcoves that had been used as commercial gates. Now converted into sandbagged ammo dumps. Exercise areas. Barracks. Emergency triage.

She doesn't know where Michelle is. Wonders about it. But not enough to ask.

Athena's fuckin tired. Wrecked. Doesn't remember how much sleep she's gotten, but it ain't much. Maybe a handful of hours over the last few days.

So fuck it. If these pukes wanna give her a place to rest, she'll take it.

Ben leads her and Dogmeat to the back room of a KSL News station in the airport. The spot that used to be a supply closet. Now it's home to a full bed.

Makes Athena think of a prison cell.

Not that there's anything inherently vile about it.

But this is what they're using to impress the Hellcat driver. A single, windowless room with a bed.

Ben says, "Nobody'll bother you here."

Athena sits on the bed. Thumbs open her whiskey. "You hiding me away?"

Ben cocks an eye. "If you need something, ask one of the troopers. They'll point you in the right direction."

He turns away. Heads off to do whatthefuckever.

Athena kicks the door closed behind him. Locks it.

Dogmeat sniffs the big bed. Hops up. Follows his tail twice then curls up at the bottom of the bed.

Athena grips the edge of the bed. Sits her ass down near the pooch. Sits cross-legged on the tiled floor. Her leathers squeak.

Dogmeat tucks his nose under his tail.

Athena holds the whiskey up. "Think I've got four bottles left." She rubs her forehead. "That is massively depressing." She sighs. Drinks. Digs into her leather jacket to find a pack of cigarettes. Does. Sparks one. "And five days of smokes."

Dogmeat whines and yawns at the same time. "Arryaoww." Slumps back on the bed. Reaches a paw out toward the Hellcat driver.

She bats it away. "Yeah, I know." Stands. Checks the lock on the door. Listens for a moment for the choppers and APCs. Their engines.

Can't see the damn things but she hears it all.

Salt Lake City is a busy hub for the Republic.

Athena works her way to her feet. Muscles complaining. Bottle in hand. Cigarette tucked between her lips. She knocks on a side door. Some flimsy thing.

No response.

She grabs the handle. Opens the door.

Mother of fuck.

There's a full bathroom.

Athena is immediately suspicious. She tests the toilet. Flushes. Twists the knobs on the sink. Checks how hot the water in the shower gets.

Pretty fuckin hot.

. . .Sonuvabitch.

Athena runs her fingers through her close-cropped blonde hair. Rubs her eyes. Sets the bottle of booze on the tank of the toilet.

She strips down in a hurry. Stands naked in front of the mirror.

The cuts and gashes across her body sting as scabs are pulled away with her leathers.

Athena steps into the shower. Smiles when the hot water hits her skin. Grime falls from her. Makes the water at her feet a little grey. Dirty. It mixes with the red from her bullet wounds. All those holes she's been sucking pain killers to get away from.

Takes her ten minutes to get clean.

She spends another half hour warm. Figures the Republic can afford the cost of her being comfortable.

Athena walks outta the shower. No towel.

She lets the cool air of the room dry her. Mouths the bottle of whiskey. Wanders toward her bed.

Dogmeat lifts his head.

Athena lights her final cigarette of the night. Looks at the dog. "You can't care that I'm naked."

Dogmeat huffs. Buries his face in his tail again.

"Right." Athena takes another pull from the bottle. She grabs the blankets and shoves herself under. Kicks her legs till Dogmeat moves his fuzzy self away from her feet.

She goes to sleep telling herself to think about the redwoods.

Her mind succumbs to the idea of safety.

What the Salt Lake airport is supposed to be.

Safe.

Safe with four walls and a dog and some whiskey.

Random gunshots *crack* through the early morning outside.

9.

Athena blinks against her pillow. Stretches. Bumps against the significant bulk of Dogmeat.

No way to tell what time it is. No windows. Safe guess is mid-afternoon.

She can usually fall into a drunken fit of sleep and stay passed out for seven or eight hours. So that's the idea she's operating under.

Athena reaches for her cigarettes. Fires one up.

Dogmeat jumps off the bed. Sits near the door.

Athena breathes smoke. Stretches again. Tells the canine, "I know. I know." She stands. Still naked. "Me first though." Stumbles into the bathroom. Sits on the toilet. Squeezes out some piss and a bowel movement.

She dresses. Straps on her Springfield Armory 1911.

Cigarette smoke trails is wisps over her shoulder as she makes her way back out to the airport.

The stares from NCR troopers haven't died down much.

Athena returns the looks. Doesn't engage otherwise.

Dogmeat trots alongside her.

She's surprised he hasn't let loose his bladder. Taken a shit on the shiny floors.

He waits till they get back out on the tarmac.

Athena admires his patience. Dog's definitely got more than her.

The Hellcat sits where she parked it in the morning. Weak sunlight glinting off the metal. Glass still shattered in places. Bullet holes still ugly. Part of her is glad the Republic mechanics haven't touched it, even though she'd be thrilled if they could do some body work.

But fuck it.

The Dodge can still roar and charge through anyone dumb enough to go toe-to-toe with Athena.

There are a few crates near the trunk. Supplies. Ammo boxes. One is MREs. Another is 40mm grenades. Rounds of .45 bullets for her 1911. Shotgun shells. A few bottles of whiskey. Water.

Athena grunts. Moves the boxes of explosives and .45 rounds over to the passenger seat. Does the same with a satchel she hasn't checked yet. The rest goes in the trunk.

Two helicopters *whumpwhumpwhump* overhead. The cannons under their cockpits thunder. They're pointed south. Toward the heart of Salt Lake City. The rounds scream off. Fast as hell. There are eruptions of smoke. Then the sound of explosions.

Athena mutters to herself. A mockery of what Ben was spouting before. "*Nyah nyah, we get attacked but we always win.* Better watch that shit, bucko."

Another explosion *booms* through the air.

But the choppers ain't shot shit.

Athena perks her ears up. Listens. Keeps her eyeballs to the south.

A new cloud of smoke billows up into the sky. A fat pillar of blackness. This one's massive. And close. A lot closer than whatever the choppers had opened fire on before.

Athena thinks: *That probably ain't good.*

Something buzzes. Chitters.

Buzzes?

Yeah.

There's the grating sound of shuddering buzzing to the south. A bee or a wasp right next to your head. But amplified a thousand times.

A rocket zooms overhead. One of the gunships jukes outta the way.

Right into the path of a second missile.

Athena instinctively ducks her head.

A fireball engulfs the chopper. A veil of yellow and orange. The vehicle smokes and spins. It twirls to the side. Impacts on the airstrip some distance away. A horrid burning wreckage.

The second attack helicopter dips its blades forward. Goes on a strafing run against whatever monster waits to the south. Its cannon goes *buddabudda.*

Alarms pierce the air. Klaxons all around the NCR's operating base.

Troopers on the tarmac break into a run. More gunships lift off.

Athena throws open the Hellcat. Snaps her fingers at Dogmeat.

The canine hops in the backseat. Licks his chops. Looks like he wants to fuckin book it.

Athena nods. "Yeah, me too. Can't yet though." Closes the door and locks the car.

She needs to talk to Oliver. Or Ben. Find Michelle.

Fuck.

Heavy weapons fire fills the sky. Rockets and bullets that go both ways.

Athena growls. "What the fuck am I doing." She jogs back into the terminal. The opposite direction most soldiers are headed.

She shouts as they blow by her. "Where's Corporal Whitmore? Sergeant Bradley?" None of their faces are focused on hers.

It ain't panic. They just don't care about her. They have shit to do.

She gets that, but the ordeal annoys the fuck outta her anyway.

Athena grabs the next trooper who nears. A young woman. Curls her fingers into fists around the chick's uniform lapels. "Where the fuck is Sergeant Bradley?"

The woman shoves Athena.

Athena punches her in the face. "Where is he."

The woman sneers. "Probably back on his fuckin bird, you crazy bitch."

Athena grunts. Turns tail. Jogs with the others back to the airstrip. Leaves the pissed-off female soldier to stew and collect herself. Takes only a heartbeat to disappear among the throngs of NCR men and women en route to their stations.

She hits the tarmac at a dead run. Looks for Oliver's C-130J. Doesn't see just it, but a dozen other cargo haulers all taking to the sky. They head west.

The NCR is spooked.

They're bailing. Leaving her.

And that makes Athena real fuckin uncomfortable.

What the fuck is dangerous enough to spook the pompous, confident NCR?

She throws herself into the Hellcat's driver seat. Turns the engine over. Watches the fuel meter jump. Likes the fact that someone apparently filled up her gas tank.

Another C-130J takes off.

Athena pounds the steering wheel. Screams. "Dirty *fucks*."

Since she doesn't have the luxury of flying, she's stuck driving south. Right toward whatever nightmare has sent the NCR into DEFCON 1.

She grabs her M79 grenade launcher. Loads a fresh boom-boom from the crate. Does the same with the sawed-off shotgun and checks the mag in her Springfield.

Doesn't plan on shooting though.

Gets the feeling the drive's gonna be hard enough without someone to assist on reloads.

And where the hell is Michelle, anyway?

If Oliver's "probably" on his plane, Michelle *probably* is too.

No way he's gonna give up the pregnant broad with the healthy baby.

Athena sniffs. "Taking a shit all over my plans."

She looks south. Grabs her damaged binoculars. Stares through the one working lens.

There's a. . .building teetering.

No. Scratch that. Not a building.

It's an animal. A titan that walks. A goddamn bug. Six massive legs. Black. Ruddy brown membranous wings folded back.

The shape makes Athena think of an ant. Big head with bulging masses of compound eyes and long antennae. A thorax that pinches down and a fat ass with a stinger.

There are raiders riding it. Controlling it.

Athena grumbles. "Hell."

How the Iron Cross fuckos managed to secure and tame a thirty-foot tall, ninety-foot long beast like that, she has no idea. But they did. And the NCR's desire to get outta town makes a lot more sense.

Athena grips the wheel. Guns the engine. Tears down the tarmac.

Dogmeat pants in the backseat. Whines.

Another explosion blossoms to the south. This one produces a small mushroom cloud near the outskirts of Salt Lake City airport.

Athena licks her lips. "All right."

We got big bugs and *mini-nukes.*

She turns the wheel to avoid NCR troopers. Military vehicles meant to deal death to Iron Cross scum. The Hellcat rolls along the airport's eastern service roads.

Gunships pound the big bug ahead. Its wings flutter, but it never takes off. Maybe too heavy. Athena doesn't know or care. Just wants to get clear.

Key problem is that the fucker won't die.

Just shakes off rounds from the helicopter cannons. Exoskeleton and appendages leaking white-yellow ichor. If anything, the sonuvabitch gets more aggressive the more damaged it is.

Another mushroom cloud mushrooms.

Athena grits her teeth. Blows through a parking lot that houses Republic vehicles in various stages of repair. Rumbles over the southernmost bridge. Crosses the river.

The insect's close now.

One of its spindly legs crashes down on the other side of I-80. Black and coated in coarse hair. Raiders on the monster's back whoop and point at the Hellcat. They throw bombs that detonate behind the Dodge and tear up chunks of the interstate.

Athena stomps the gas. Pushes the Hellcat up to a hundred. One-twenty. The road becomes a beige and grey blur. The trundling bug shrinks in the rearview.

Gunships keep the fire on.

Rockets burst against its dark flanks. Send chitin sloughing off in fat clumps.

A trio of Iron Cross pickups peel away from their lumbering pal. Attempt to give chase. Crazed goons in the beds tote machine guns. Their weapons fire wild.

Athena grabs for the grenade launcher. Sets it in her lap.

Raider goobers wanna play tag, fine. She's it.

She's the queen bitch of fuck mountain.

The Hellcat roars.

Athena watches the rearview.

The big bug stops just outside the airport. Throws its head up.

There's a tremendous flash of white light that blinds Athena.

She squints. Tries to keep her eyes on the asphalt ahead. Foot on the gas. The shape of the road is a smudge, but she stays between the shoulders. "Living fuck."

Dogmeat wails.

The insane rumble of the bomb rattles the Dodge and the driver's guts.

Athena's vision recovers. Ghosts of the flash remain in the corners of her eyeballs, but she can see. Mostly.

A behemoth of a mushroom cloud expands behind her. The insect evaporates. Body torn apart and disintegrated. The land around it pulses with nuclear force. The blast radius expands with blazing speed. The roads and greenery explode. Burst into flames. Become dust.

The Iron Cross assholes in pursuit are dashed apart. Ragdolls on a murderous wave of energy. Their trucks shatter. Their bodies melt away.

Only the Hellcat could get to speed fast enough. Outrun the distant but deadly atom-split.

She keeps the Dodge in the red. Pushes the car hard. Doesn't slow till she gets near The Great Salt Lake. She guides the car to the side of the road. Rubs her face. Watches the mushroom cloud dissipate.

Athena sighs. Blinks. Breathes through her nose. Holds her head.

She punches the steering wheel. The car's horn bleats.

Athena rests her head in her hands. Massages her temples.

She bites her lower lip and looks back at Dogmeat.

The canine pants without end. Can't relax.

Yeah. Seems about right.

Athena lights a cigarette. Grimaces when she tries to take a deep breath. She steps outta the Hellcat. Looks around at. . .nothing.

There's nothing.

Just pavement. Soil too dosed with salt to grow anything. A creek.

She frowns.

Dogmeat buries his snout under his paws. His eyes meet hers.

Athena says, "Yeah."

10.

Athena heads west. Only thing she can do.

The nuke was the Iron Cross set off seems to have ruined the army they brought.

Nobody follows her.

She passes a lake. Winds up between some salt flats.

And for a while, the salt flats don't stop. White expanses that surround her and Dogmeat. The white expanses become peppered by rocky brown mountains. Nothing like the Rockies, but mountains nonetheless.

A rusty white sign with blue lettering welcomes her and Dogmeat to Nevada.

Moments later, it's casino after fuckin casino.

More rocks. More dust.

The lack of anything interesting to look at shoves Athena into her own mind.

She wonders about the insect. Wonders how the Iron Cross could be able to do such a thing and catch the NCR by surprise.

Or did they. . . .

NCR pukes like Ben made it sound like the Republic is always up for a good fight. But the cargo planes were bugging out as soon as the first gunship went down.

Alarms blaring.

Seemed like they were ready to go.

And nobody let Athena know.

She wonders if she got so drunk. . .Well, wonders if she was *too* drunk and exhausted to be woken up. It's possible. Oliver certainly made it seem as though she and her leg—the rotten curse of Frankie's tech—were important.

Maybe not as important as getting a healthy baby away from the nuclear terror the Iron Cross brought to bear on the NCR's Salt Lake base, though.

Athena shakes her head.

So this Western Devil cocksmoker is willing to use nuclear suicide squads to kill her and the New California Republic is willing to run under the assumption Athena can take care of herself.

Can't blame Oliver *or* the stuffy colonel for making that decision.

She doesn't need to fuckin *like* it, but she can't blame em for it.

After all, what she's most pissed about is maybe losing Michelle as a meal ticket.

Athena drives. Smokes.

She pulls off into a tiny town. Sign says RYNDON overtop DEVILS GATE.

Delightful.

Athena's just looking to take a break someplace quiet. Have a breather. Maybe grab a carton of smokes.

But the place is *too* quiet.

She ain't even sure it counts as a town.

There's a single red-roofed country store. Some houses. Dead vehicles.

Athena lets Dogmeat out so he can sniff around. Maybe scare up an animal she can murder and cook. Then rummages through what the NCR left for her by the car.

Nothing shocking there. But the satchel has some goodies stuffed inside. Like a map similar to the one Oliver was looking at on the C-130J. It laden with markings that show NCR bases and stash houses. A badge for "NCR | Beale AFB" and a bronze star. A hand-written list of radio frequencies and channels the Republic is active on. A Midland two-way radio.

Athena grunts.

Maybe Oliver and Ben didn't quite leave her for dead after all.

She turns the walkie-talkie on. Full charge. Tunes it to the NCR's emergency broadcast channel. Listens to the hiss. Clips it to the zipper pocket on the chest of her leather jacket. She marches toward the country store. Pistol in its holster on her right side. Sawed-off on the left.

Dogmeat barks. He's down the road a little. In front of the dingy depot. Whatever's got his hackles up, it's inside the store.

Athena grips her 1911. Holds it out in front of her, barrel pointed at the ground.

A shot rings out. Two.

One bullet ricochets off the dusty ground near Dogmeat's front left paw.

The second punches into the canine's torso.

Dogmeat cries out. Flops to the side. Holds himself up with shaky legs.

Athena shouts. Roars. Rushes toward the front of the store. Her stance wide-legged like a linebacker.

She tucks herself against some cover near the doors. Low. Sees they're barricaded with planks of wood. A small window to the side where the jackasses were shooting from waits open and now unattended.

Athena pulls her shotgun. Barks at the occupant or occupants: "You just *fucked up*." She aims the double-barrel sawed-off at the seam between the doors. Pounds the barricade there with twin loads of buckshot.

Wood splinters. Cracks.

The Hellcat driver reloads. Rears back. Kicks the damaged doors off their hinges with the brute power of her robotic right leg.

She sees a man and a teenage girl suddenly cast into the afternoon light of the day. Yellow rays push into the gloom of the store. Expose the skin and bone condition of both survivors.

They're dangerously thin. Eyes desperate and afraid. The dried-out pelts of small rodents hang from empty shelves.

Probably thought Dogmeat would be good eating.

Bad move.

The gaunt man tightens his grip on the AR-15 rifle in his hands.

Athena doesn't give him a chance. Buckshot slams into his chest. Shreds his skin. Sends specks of blood splattering all around.

He falls back into empty cardboard boxes.

The teenage girl scurries away. Dog tags around her neck on a ball chain jingle and chime. She doesn't cry out at the sudden violent death of whoever this asshole was. She scrambles out the door. Tattered clothing flaps in the wind.

And those dog tags keep on jingling and chiming while the dust flies around her feet.

Makes Athena wonder when the last time she saw dog tags was. Dog tags that weren't around the neck of military personnel who'd dropped dead in New York City, anyway. With nobody around to take the tags to anyone who might give a shit.

But, hell, not even the NCR uses dog tags anymore. They've got their badges and their stars.

Also makes Athena wonder if there wasn't something absolutely awful happening here. And part of her wants to call after the girl. Tell the girl to stop. She can help.

She doesn't.

She sniffs. Groans. Walks around the big counter at the front of the store. She steps over the dead guy's legs. Plays her eyes along his splayed form. The wetness at his crotch from when he pissed himself at death.

The AR-15 he'd clung to lies like unused garbage by his bloody carcass. It ain't even worth salvaging.

Athena roots around near the long-dead cash register. Seeks out cartons or packs of cigarettes. Finds a few Winstons. A carton of Marlboro Reds.

They'll do.

She turns and heads back outside.

Dogmeat's there. Waiting. His ears pointed up. Fluffy party hats. His tail wags as Athena approaches.

Athena cocks an eye. Stops in her tracks. A smile flirts with her lips. But her concern is mostly directed at what the hell is going on.

She furrows her brow. Says to Dogmeat, "You're chipper for a pooch with a bullet in his gut."

He barks. Follows her to the Hellcat.

She shoves the ill-gotten smokes into the trunk. Pats Dogmeat on his rump. Takes a knee. Checks his sides with careful fingers.

There oughtta be blood but there ain't. The garbage rifle the asshole used on him fired .223 or 5.56 rounds. The bullet should have plowed right through the dog. Carved a leaky canal in his flesh.

Instead, she finds a hole in Dogmeat's fat and fur. She touches the wound. There's a miniscule amount of red *there*. But underneath. . . .

Athena parts the pooch's hair so she can see.

Metal underneath.

Athena grunts. "So. . .What? That bullet just knocked the wind outta you? Cuz it sure as shit didn't drive through those chrome bones of yours." She scratches Dogmeat behind the ears. "But I figure you gotta be mostly dog under all that. You're too goofy to be a murder machine."

Dogmeat barks.

"Yeah, all right." Athena scrounges up a can of Chef Boyardee Beefaroni. Pauses before opening it. "Hang on."

Dogmeat sits on his haunches.

Athena decides it's endlessly stupid to keep doing this. She wanders back to the rotten store. Walks between the empty aisles. Finally finds a double-sided dog bowl. One bowl for food and the other for water.

She holds it up for Dogmeat to see when she returns to the car.

He stands. Barks. Wags his tail.

Definitely seems to recognize what it's for.

Athena plants it on the ground near the Hellcat. Tilts the Beefaroni can so its contents *splortch* out into one of the bowls. She does the same with a bottle of Poland Spring water.

Dogmeat feasts.

Athena smirks. Plucks the radio from its spot on her jacket. She turns up the volume. Still just static. Then starts to scan through the other channels.

She thinks maybe the NCR or someone else might be broadcasting shit she wants to hear.

Her mind bounces over to memories of Michelle doing the same with her hand crank radio.

Athena scratches her cheek. Vaguely annoyed at the thought.

A boom thunders off to the east. Something big. She wonders if it was another nuke. Or an NCR gunship going on the offensive.

Athena pushes the walkie-talkie's buttons. Scans through the channels. Does this with one hand while she lights a cigarette with the other.

She grimaces. Spits.

Damn cancer stick is way past its "best by" date. Stale and more unpleasant than usual but. . .still capable of delivering that precious nicotine to her bloodstream.

So far on the radio: bupkis.

"Fuckin two-way radios like this are always worthless," Athena says. "Companies sell plastic pieces of crap while boasting they have a range of twenty or thirty miles and then the fine print says you'll only get that kinda distance on a flat fuckin plain in 'optimal conditions.' Christ." She clips the radio back into place.

Dogmeat gives not one shit about this. He finishes his food. His water. Walks in a circle three times and lies down with a huff.

Athena takes a deep breath. Braces herself for the new pain that comes with that. Grits her teeth. Mutters to herself. "We keep heading west." She taps the roof of the Hellcat. "Just get back on I-80 and keep heading west."

And hope she doesn't run outta gas.

Might run into that loopy teenage girl along the way.

Athena's brain snaps at her: *So?*

It's a fair question.

One she doesn't have any satisfactory way to respond to.

So she slides behind the wheel. Guns the engine. Grinds asphalt.

Next town over is big enough to have its own airport, but there's no sign of any NCR planes or helicopters. No sign of anything at all.

Athena and Dogmeat roll on.

She smokes and mouths a bottle of whiskey. Keeps her speed up for ten miles. Twenty. She sees signs for "Central Carlin." Has no idea what Carlin is and can't be bothered to care.

Starts to grate on her how brown and boring the goddamn landscape is. She tries to find some interest in the rolling hills. The little canyons.

Can't.

They end up in a rocky little spot named Emigrant. Like half the other places around here, it doesn't consist of much. This time, just a looped road off the interstate and about six ranch houses that seem to have been converted from trailer park homes arranged in a circle.

She parks in the center. Waits to see if any psychos are gonna rush out to get the car.

Nope.

Nothing here but stones and the occasional dirt devil.

That crap, and a spider web in the doorway of one of the converted trailer homes. The arachnid at the center is the size of a Chihuahua.

Athena opts to keep the car doors closed.

She punches through the radio channels again. Hopes to land on something—anything.

Hope is a dangerous thing.

She tries the Hellcat's radio. Sets it to seek a signal.

While it runs through frequencies, she reaches into the satchel that was left for her. Unfolds the map from inside. Looks over the markings of stash houses and cleared towns. Tries to find an NCR-friendly camp. One that's close.

Reno.

Reno.

She searches on the map for the legend. Little lines that'll explain the distances. The scale of the map. She compares her fingers to the lines. Best match she's got is the width of her thumb more or less equaling a mile.

Then begins the annoying and arduous task of *thumbing* her route along I-80. Trying to calculate the miles.

Two-hundred and sixty times.

She presses her thumb against this stupid fuckin map *two-hundred and sixty times*.

Athena leans her head back against the driver's seat. Lights a cigarette. Chugs some whiskey.

There are choppers up there somewhere nearby. Their engines thrumming and echoing across the great dusty nothingness.

She blinks.

Thinks: *Well, guess I could always succumb to death* here. *In goddamn Emigrant.*

She leans forward. Doesn't like that idea at all. Blows smoke.

Hellcat gets 22 highway miles-to-the-gallon. Optimally. She shaves that to 20. Tank size is supposed to be 18.5, and she's near half from gunning it and trying to outrun a nuke. She assumes she's got nine gallons left.

That's 180. Not enough.

Athena checks out the windows. Makes sure there's no cranky kinda bug that wants to snack on her. Steps out. Checks the supplies in the trunk.

Two ten-gallon drums stare up at her.

She nods. "All right."

Question now is: Does she burn through sundown to get to Reno?

Athena cracks her neck.

No question the Iron Cross want her ass. If anything, they're more into the full-fledged fuckin insanity than ever. Headlights at night are gonna make the Hellcat show up like a damn flare.

She wonders how a nuclear explosion at night would look.

Frowns.

Probably very pretty.

The spider in the door way shudders with the breeze.

Athena palms a bottle of water. Slams the trunk shut. Pops a painkiller and throws some Poland Spring behind it.

She watches the spider for another moment. Notices that it's perfectly content to let the wind rock it from side to side. And wait for some baseball-sized fly or moth to wander into its trap.

"We'll be gone soon." Athena takes a swig of whiskey. Frowns. "We'll be gone soon and you and your gazillion-legged freak friends can have the whole planet."

She can imagine the mutant bear from the Rockies ambling along. Sniffing piss forever.

Ain't as though humans have done much better.

11.

Static.

Twenty miles of static from the Hellcat's radio and the walkie-talkie as the sun sinks toward the horizon.

Athena finds herself somewhere outside a Halliburton plant. Can't see much. The skeletons of metal struts and structures. A few random lanterns burning atop scaffolds and lookout points.

Place like that having a living, active population is probably not something that's gonna work in her favor.

The Hellcat's radio stops seeking a signal. Lands on one.

Nightmare sounds. Screams. Liquid falling. Then voices. A gravel-gargling voice escapes from the Hellcat's speakers.

". . .There's the bitch. *Get the Hellbitch.*" Laughter. "Hi there, Hellbitch."

Athena rolls her head around on her neck.

Of course the lunatics are hiding out at a Halliburton facility. Wouldn't make sense if the sadistic goons didn't.

Headlights come into view behind her.

She plays with the trigger of the M79 grenade launcher. Just fingers it.

More than two hundred miles left till she gets somewhere the NCR might be.

Hundred and fifty miles till she needs refuel.

What are the odds anyone makes it to their goal?

Athena feels in her pocket for the uppers she stole from Mark. That military pharmaceutical wonder pill. Real nice with its ability to threaten a heart attack but make you an energized, hardcore killer.

She chews one between her teeth. Crunches it. Rolls down the driver side window. Watches the rearview. The dozen yellow and white beams that cut through the darkness behind her.

Six trucks.

Athena clicks her tongue. Aims the grenade launcher behind her. "Wish these dickheads would leave me alone." Thumps off a round.

The 40mm grenade is a hammer blow to the closest Iron Cross truck. It lands right on the hood. Forces the front of the vehicle down. So it skitters and plants its frame in the asphalt. Bursts into flames. Flips the same way some idiot doing gymnastics does.

Athena sets her jaw. Doesn't even understand why these stupid suicide hamsters wanna give chase at this point.

. . .*Really.*

She yells out the window. "I'm sorry I hurt your feelings." Steers with her left hand. Opens the thumper with her right and shakes out the used shell. "Learn to appreciate the healing process."

Athena catches Dogmeat's eye. The pooch doing his usual thing and hiding his snout under his paws. She says, "Hang tight, pupper." Reloads.

The gravelly voice on the radio keeps the banter going. "We don't wanna hurt you yet. Why don't you slow down? Put the boom-booms away?" Laughter. "The Devil *really* wants to meet you."

Athena grunts. "Glad I'm such a popular gal."

She aims behind her. Lets fly with another grenade.

Another truck crumples and explodes in hellfire.

Athena sets the M79 on the passenger seat. Unclips the walkie-talkie from her jacket. Clicks over to the NCR's emergency channel. "Dunno if there are any of you assholes out there listening, but I could use a hand." She releases the talk button.

Static is the response.

There's movement to her right in one of the many dusty, expansive fields.

It's a bug. Big one. It stands out against the beige rocky backdrop in the dying light of the day. The damn thing's legs piston up and down in broad sweeps. Massive mandibles click. Glossy, translucent wings shudder.

Athena groans. "You gotta be fuckin kidding." She pushes the Dodge harder. Gets it to one-sixty. "How many of these things do they have?"

She gets back on the radio. Yells into the NCR's frequency. "There's nuclear bugfuck. . .fucker. . .outside. I'm near—" She has no idea where she is geographically. Everything looks the same outside. "Someone's gonna need to deal with this thing. Send a gunship."

Then she tosses the walkie-talkie into the passenger seat. Can't be bothered to fiddle with it anymore.

Useless hunk of plastic.

The Hellcat's roaring across the asphalt fast enough now that the Iron Cross can't keep up. But it also means she's burning a helluva lot more gas.

Takes plenty of fuel to feed this V8 beast.

Radio in the dash comes alive in a sing-song. That Iron Cross weirdo. "We're gonna geeet you. We're gonna geeet you. We're gonna geeet you."

The road curves ahead.

Athena pumps the brakes.

The insect nears I-80. Turns its big bulbous head and those shiny eyes to focus on her. Antennae on its noggin jitter. Flick from side to side. The raiders on its back hoist up chemical sticks. Lanterns. Torches.

It makes Athena think of a terminally bizarre lightshow. Or rave.

The raider on the radio giggles. "Oh, come *on*, Hellcat. Aren't you bored yet? Just. . .accept it. *Let it happen.*" He hisses. "The Devil's gonna get you. And he's gonna put new holes in you. And he'll keep you alive while you scream and squeal. And he'll slide all *kinds* of things into you."

Athena punches the power button on the radio in the dash. "Holy shit, shut up." Looks in the rearview at the silhouette of the enormous critter behind.

She wonders if the titanic bug can catch up to her. If it gets tired. Has to stop.

The *how* of how the Iron Cross are able to control it doesn't concern her. It's here. It's happening. And she needs something significantly more powerful than an M79 grenade launcher to deal with it.

The walkie-talkie in the passenger seat clicks. Buzzes.

A man says: "Coming in hot."

A woman chimes in right after: "Very hot."

Athena squints. Turns her gaze up into the evening sky through the front windshield.

Two shapes there. Both attack choppers. Their blades a whirling blur. Lights on their noses and bellies blink.

Missiles streak away from pods on their sides. Four bright flashes. Four trails of smoke and accelerant.

They zoom high above the Hellcat's roof. Explode in glorious fireballs against the big bug's head. Turn its many-lensed eyes into chunks that pop out and squish against the asphalt.

The rockets crack its mandibles. Its face.

Raiders fall away. Some ablaze. Some jump to avoid any more missiles. All knocked around by the concussive blasts.

The bug teeters and totters. Wobbles. Its legs go slack. The incredible bulk of its body slams against the ground. More insectoid white-yellow gore erupts from the holes in its chitin.

Athena braces herself for another nuclear explosion. Closes her eyes against the blinding light she's anticipating.

Nothing comes.

No nuke.

She cackles. Smacks the steering wheel. "Well *fuuuuuuck you*." She slows the Hellcat. Snaps up the walkie-talkie. "Who'm I talking to? You guys with the New California Republic?"

The woman's voice says: "No. It was in our best interest."

The man says: "There's been too much raider activity here recently."

"It used to be nice and quiet."

Athena wrinkles her nose. Like she smells something foul. "Oh. . .kay."

The man says: "Look for Battle Mountain Airport."

The woman says: "It's up the road. We'll meet you there."

Athena considers this. ". . .Sure." Clips the walkie-talkie to her jacket again. Looks back at Dogmeat. "What do we think about this?"

Dogmeat's eyebrows flit from side to side. He sits up. Whines. "Yeah. Strange motherfuckers."

12.

Athena's having a hard time keeping track of how many factions there are out here.

On the east coast, you had little fiefdoms of dickheads. Apocalyptic barons who wanted to control their areas. Have some fun. Make some money. Fuck someone or some*thing* new and exciting.

Midwest was. . .well, Bugtown. A real irradiated wasteland with rock & roll beamed outta Columbus, Ohio by the deformed Dapper brothers. The Trakers ran crude up from Texas. The Wraiths went after the Trakers' supplies.

She's not sure she can count the Rocky Rangers as real power players. They seemed more like the east coasters. Content to hold onto Denver and keep their shit tight.

Now there's the New California Republic. A real military organization. One that claims it's taking the wastes back. Supposed "good guys." And the Iron Cross—which scares the shit outta Athena given how vast their network seems to be.

Now there's. . .whoever the fuck is holding down Battle Mountain.

Only thing she figures is that they can't be total cocksuckers if they blew up the bug.

Athena admits to herself that that ain't much to go by. Who *would* want a giant insect creeping around in their backyard? But she's trusted some people with more for less.

Like Bullhorn.

That poor sonuvabitch.

Makes her wonder where Sherlock is.

If the kid's head is in a box on the Western Devil's goddamn mantelpiece somewhere.

That's what she thinks about while she follows a dilapidated little side road along I-80. Sun all the way sunken now. The Hellcat's headlights catch puffs of dust and tumbleweeds along the way.

Far off to the side is the airport. Tiny for what it is. Just a handful of stout buildings. Hangars with the lights on.

The two attack choppers *whumpwhumpwhump* in the night sky. They settle themselves on two pads next to each other in the middle of the airport proper. Right across the tarmac.

Athena passes by two relics from bygone wars—fighter planes—as she drives the Hellcat in and parks next to the central office building.

She waits, as she always does, to see what's gonna greet her before she vacates the comfort of her car.

But there's nothing. Just the lights on the runways. The whine of the two helicopters' engines dying down. The spinning blades slow.

The pilots pop their cockpit doors. Hop out. Saunter across the airstrip a couple hundred feet away. The man and the woman. They're both in flight suits. Pistols on their thighs. Round helmets with visors that make em look a bit like insects themselves.

Athena licks her lips. Taps the steering wheel with fidgety fingers.

Figures: *Fuck it*.

She opens her door. Steps out. Raises a hand to stop Dogmeat from bounding onto the tarmac.

The canine barks.

Athena shakes her head. *Wait*. "I don't want you getting shot again."

Dogmeat grumbles. Growls. Makes a noise like *grrrrrmmp*.

Athena slams the driver's side door. Turns to face the pilots. Keeps her hands near the weapons at her sides as she walks out toward em.

They remove their helmets.

Both are Hispanic. Around Athena's age. Mid-forties. Dark hair. Eyes. Complexion.

They offer her a wave. Hold their headgear with one hand near their hips.

Athena nods. Stops when she thinks she's still close enough to the Hellcat to scramble away *and* get a few good shots in on the pilots if they start any shit. "Thanks for. . .Well, thanks for blowing that creepy-crawly to hell."

The man and the woman halt. Keep about twenty feet between themselves and Athena. The two being cautious as well.

She's not sure how to take that.

Might be her reputation as a violent bitch proceeds her.

The woman says, "It was in our best interests to kill the tarantula hawk."

Athena blinks. "The. . .hawk?"

The pilots' speech patterns are rapid-fire. Not quite talking over one another but close.

She says: "It's a wasp named the tarantula hawk."

He says: "State insect of New Mexico, strangely."

"It's fairly docile."

"Far as wasps go."

"Major assholes, far as insects go."

"The female's sting is ludicrously painful."

"Literal professional, scientific advice if you got stung was to lie in a ditch and scream."

"It would hurt so badly that you might run off and get yourself dead."

"Go crazy. Better to cry till it passes."

The two pilots smile.

Athena furrows her brow. Tries to be inoffensive but can't help it. "There something wrong with you guys? Cuz that is *really* annoying."

They both frown.

He says: "No, we're fine."

She says: "We're twins."

"Juan."

"Juana."

Athena cocks an eyebrow. "Right." She shifts her weight from one foot to the other. Tries to figure out why they wanted her to come back here. "You said you're not with the New California Republic?"

Juana shakes her head. "No."

"You're the only pilots I've seen who aren't NCR."

"Well."

Juan says, "We used to be."

"At the start of it."

"Then we left."

"And took our choppers with us."

Athena rests her right hand on the butt of her 1911. Doesn't pull it but wants it ready to go. She says, "Why?"

Juana casts a sideways glance at Juan. Returns her gaze to Athena. "The New California Republic wants control."

Juan says, "Reclamation is control."

"You become part of the NCR."

"The NCR becomes your purpose."

"Your life."

"You reason to *be* alive."

"There's no freedom under the Founders."

"It's all about *control.*"

Athena finds herself in the intensely bizarre position of wanting to defend the assholes who bailed on her. "You'd rather the Iron Cross was in charge?"

The twins are silent for a moment.

Juana says, "We'd rather nobody was."

Juan says, "We'd rather be left to do what we want."

Athena grunts. "I'm. . .gonna go." She points a lazy finger at the Hellcat. "Thanks again. You guys just." Thumbs-up. "Keep on doing you."

She thinks: *What the fuck am I doing?*

Juan stops her with a shout. "Wait, why are you looking for the NCR?"

Athena squints. "They've got something of mine."

Juana says, "We can help you."

Juan says, "We've got a long-range transmitter."

"Reno is the closest NCR controlled territory."

"Radio should reach there."

"And we can make you some dinner."

The twins smile.

Athena's face is stone. "So here's how this is gonna happen." She pulls her 1911. Her sawed-off shotgun. "I'm gonna keep my guns out. I'm gonna keep em on you two. You're gonna take me to that transmitter. You're gonna put me in touch with the NCR. Then we're gonna part ways."

Juan frowns. "You don't want dinner?"

"Not hungry." She shakes her Springfield Armory .45. "Let's go."

The twins look to one another. Shrug. They cut a wide path around Athena and her weapons. March without much hesitation toward the central office door.

Athena drops the sawed-off into its wide holster. Uses her key fob to lock the Hellcat.

Which sends Dogmeat's ears straight up in confusion.

He doesn't wanna be locked in the damn car.

She trains her 1911 on the pilots. Shuffles the barrel from Juan to Juana. Always pointed at their backs. Where she thinks she might be able to slam a .45 somewhere in their spine and take em outta the fight.

Athena smiles at the thought.

A fat .45 slug shoving itself between their vertebrae.

She's not even sure why that makes her happy. Or pleases her. Or why her brain considers it an option.

Wouldn't be the worst thing she's ever done.

Athena does a cost-benefit analysis in her head while she watches the twins' flight suits jiggle with their movement.

This is what you're reduced to. An animal. Desperate. Unthinking. Unfeeling.

You pretended to be the savior of a young pregnant woman. Fought through a hundred men. But not for her.

You fought cuz you thought you could trade her and her child for the redwoods.

And now the NCR has her.

And the NCR doesn't give nearly as much of a shit about you.

And you don't have a single fuckin card left to play.

Athena can't do it.

Wants to in a sick way but can't.

Doesn't have a good enough reason to kill the oddball twins right now.

Their strangeness brings the balance close, but they also helped her.

So. . .she'll see it out.

Dapper brothers seemed wonky and horrid at first. Then they became the first and only folks she met who weren't rotten bastards.

She wonders how they are. Figures they're still getting supplies from road runners to keep the radio station on-air. Dealing with their train-wreck bodies.

The twins sidle up to the front door.

Juan holds the knob.

Athena slides under the window to the left. Peeks up to check inside to see if there are assholes waiting.

Nothing she can see except some storage boxes. A single, wide bed on rickety springs. Big desk station with electronics she figures is this radio rig they've been talking about.

Athena tells Juan: "Go in."

The man does. Continues his this-is-normal act.

Juana follows.

Athena slips in behind em. Throws herself against the wall in a defensive position. Her 1911 up. Scanning.

Whole place seems to be just one big long room with the basics like a bed. Some survival supplies in crates. The radio station.

That's what Athena cares about now.

She barks at the twins. "Crank up the radio." Gestures with the Springfield Armory handgun. "You get me on the horn with the NCR." She snaps her fingers. "Chop chop."

Juan nods. Picks up a headset at the radio station. "I'm working on it."

Juana stops near her brother. "Would you like some food?"

"It's good."

"Not radioactive."

"The meat is. . .kind of tough."

"But it tastes good in a stew."

"We make a lotta stews."

Athena sniffs. Can't smell anything beyond the crappy air and exhaust and diesel and a rot like bad meat. "Said I wasn't hungry."

She steps away from her perch. Moves a little farther into the office. Scans its yellow walls. Posters there of aircraft that don't exist anymore. Schematics whose paper is eaten away by decay. They show the American hero aircraft of World War II.

Athena doesn't care what they are.

What she cares about is the bizarre twin on the radio.

She cares about the other half of that binary system. Juana always keeping an eye on her brother. Taking her cues from the doof on the tech.

She cares about the single bed in the room. Says, "You two. . .sleep together?"

There's a pause. A lull.

Athena doesn't like that at all.

Juan says, "It gets cold here at night."

Juana says, "When you sleep with someone, you share the warmth."

"Stay warm."

"Sometimes it saves you."

Athena ain't sure how far she can walk into the office before it looks like she's snooping. Which she is. But she'd rather play it easy. "You guys. . .uh. . . ." She twirls the barrel of the 1911.

Juan turns some dials on the radio. Frowns. "It's very lonely here."

Juana tilts her head. "Nobody comes out here. Except the Iron Cross now."

"Usually it's dust and bugs."

"Or dust and some *awful person*."

Athena grunts. Keeps her 1911 up. Lets her left hand caress the grip on the sawed-off shotgun in its fat holster. In case it's needed.

And she thinks it might be.

She says, "I don't care so much that you fuck each other, all right?" She rolls her tongue around in her mouth. "But." She gets closer to the bed. Sees something she doesn't like: part of a little ball chain half-buried beneath a stained pillow. That little length of chain is the same type the girl at the country store was wearing with her dog tags.

Athena whirls on the twins. Them both standing so close to one another. She says, "I came to a little shop the other day.

Needed, uh—" she smiles. "It's dumb as hell when I say it, but I needed one of those double bowls for my dog." She plays her fingers in the air. "With the food on one side and the water on the other. And. . .I went inside this place. And there was a girl and a man. But the girl bolted. Run right the fuck off." She shrugs. "I was wondering if you'd seen her? You got those choppers and all."

Juan furrows his brow. Stares at the radio desk.

He hasn't even made an attempt to talk to anyone with that goddamn microphone in front of him.

Juana doesn't say anything either.

Athena grunts.

Snap-fires her 1911.

Puts two in Juana's chest.

Volcanoes of blood erupt under the weird woman's flight suit. Strings of red splash across her brother's shoulders. The side of his head.

He screams as she falls. Shrieks. "Oh, God. Juana." Goes for the pistol on his leg.

Athena shakes her head. "Nuh uh." Shoots Juan's hand.

Juan screams anew. Cradles the ruined mass of flesh that used to be his fingers. "*Why?* We didn't do anything to you." Tears well in his eyes.

Athena grunts. She keeps her gun on the dumb bastard at the radio. Doesn't wanna shoot him—yet—in the hopes he can get a signal out to the NCR. "The dog tag chain on the bed makes me think you saw that girl. Makes me think you did something nasty to her." She keeps the gun trained. Reaches for the chain on the bed. Pulls it free from under the pillow and holds it up. It glistens in the light. "You shoulda hid this better."

Juan cries and mumbles and grumbles.

Athena says, "I was gonna shoot you both in the back before. I'll be honest." She shrugs. "I thought it might make my life easier. But. . .I couldn't. I needed a reason. First time that's ever been an issue for me." Chuckle. "But now that's been resolved, hasn't it?"

The incestuous pilot palsies as he sobs. Tears and blood drop in equal measure.

Athena barks orders. "Get on the radio. You tell the NCR I'm here. And you tell em to come get me in one of their big birds. Something with *guns* that can level a fuckin *town.*"

Juan sniffs. Groans. "No." He shakes his head. "No, you killed Juana. I'm not gonna help you."

The Hellcat driver squints at him. "You're telling me 'No?'"

"I'm not gonna do it."

Athena nods. Bites her bottom lip. "Here are your options: Get on the radio and call the NCR. Notice how 'No' ain't in there?"

Juan rocks back and forth. "I am *not* gonna help you."

"Then I'm gonna kill you and let my dog piss on you."

The pilot sniffles. Looks down at the body of his sister. Looks up to meet Athena's eyes.

She sees hate there. Pain and sadness. But mostly hate.

Suits Athena fine. Never been in it to make friends.

She gestures with her handgun for Juan to get the fuck on with it.

He turns up the volume on a small speaker next to the radio. The room is finally filled with the buzzy hum of functional radio equipment.

Juan adjusts the dials. Settles on a frequency. He holds a button at the base of the microphone stand. Tries to steady his voice.

"This is. . . ." He releases the button. Takes a breath. Winces. Makes a whining sound.

He hits the button again. "This is Battle Mountain. Is anyone there reading me?"

The buzzy hum takes over again for about twenty seconds. During which Athena lights a cigarette and the shithead Juan weeps some more.

Then comes a voice. "Yeah, we read you."

Juan glances at Athena. Clears his throat. Hits the button. Stays quiet for a moment. Like he's trying to figure out what to say.

That Athena ain't a fan of.

Juan shouts with a rapid-fire burst of energy. "She's *here*. The Hellcat is *here*. Come and get this awful fuck—"

Athena sends a .45 slug through the side of Juan's head. Brains and bone and gore explode out the other side. They drizzle down a nearby wall. Red, lazy party streamers.

The radio comes to life with a chorus of chattering, mad voices. They sing and laugh. "Hi, Hellbitch! Hiiiiiiii! We're gonna get you! *We're gonna get you!*"

Athena rushes to the radio. Kicks Juan's slouched body away. Spins some of the dials at random so that at least she doesn't have to listen to the Iron Cross cocksmokers.

She runs out to the Hellcat. Cigarette bouncing on her lips.

She digs into the satchel for the list of NCR frequencies. Shit that's different from the walkie-talkie channels. Runs back inside. She ain't familiar with how any of this broadcasting garbage is supposed to work.

Is this ham radio? The crap turbo-nerds used to fawn over in their parents' basements.

Whole lotta buttons.

Way too goddamn many buttons.

Little bits of print on the equipment say things like "Twin PBT CLR" and "AF – RF/SQL" and "XFC" and "M.SCOPE" and *what the fuck does any of this shit mean.*

She turns the largest knob. Watches the frequency numbers on the display change. Okay. Good. She tunes it in. Finds a button that says "TRANSMIT." Makes sure that's clicked. Grabs the mic. "If anyone from the New California Republic is listening, I need to speak with Sergeant Major Oliver Bradley immediately." She pauses. "This is the Hellcat."

Athena releases the button. Smokes. Waits.

The speaker hums. Buzzes.

She taps her fingers against the desk. She doesn't have a clue how much time she's got before the Iron Cross is on her again. No way to know where the bastards Juan broadcasted to are. Even if she knew the power and the wattage of the setup here, she doesn't think she could figure out the range.

Just hopes Juan wasn't jerking off when he said it could reach the NCR.

But she's done waiting for an answer.

It's time to fuckin go.

She grabs the mic one more time. Barks. "I hope you stupid assholes are listening. I'm heading west on I-80 from Battle Mountain Airport. Right now. Bring something dangerous. I'm probably gonna have company."

Athena stands. Marches toward the door. Stops herself. Decides it's worth taking the time to see if these two weird lunatics have anything worth stealing. Turns around and heads toward the back of the building.

Ain't much here. Not even any containers to loot.

Just one more door back here. Kinda flimsy.

She kicks it in.

Eyeballs the interior.

It's a kitchen. Ad hoc. With a series of desks doing double duty as counters. A refrigerator that seems to be running. Probably connected to the same generator running the landing lights on the airstrip.

She doesn't see any cans of food, but the stench of rot is much worse in here.

And she realizes why.

The stew.

The incest twins' fuckin stew.

There are buckets of it. Literal buckets of semi-congealed slop. Ingredients not as unknown as Athena would like.

She spots articles of clothing tossed into one corner of the kitchen. Stuff the twins wouldn't wear—cuz they're made for children and toddlers and goddamn teenagers.

Athena takes a deep breath. Hates herself for a moment. A few heartbeats.

She mutters to herself as she storms away. Back toward the Hellcat. "I saved that girl from a rapist and got her turned into *fuckin stew* by incest cannibals." Holsters her 1911 and balls her fists. Smokes with angry fervor. "Never thought my goal of *dying* would be such a nightmare."

When she gets outside, she sees the choppers and wishes she could fly one of em. Make some of this a helluva lot easier.

Then again, she wishes for a lotta things that ain't ever panned out.

13.

Athena drives hard. Cares less about the gas now than she did a couple hours ago. Just wants to move like a motherfucker. Stay ahead of the Iron Cross.

She keeps whiskey in the cup holder. Cigarettes and lighter in her lap. Walkie-talkie on her jacket. The grenade launcher waits in the passenger seat for the inevitable assholes to give chase.

But nothing yet.

The only thing around her is a black sky. Blacktop. Dust and the occasional glint of insect or animal eyes in the darkness when her headlights hit em.

She blows through a town. Notices a few lanterns in a few windows.

Sure as shit doesn't stop to investigate.

Stays that way for a while. Quiet with the steady rumble of the V8 fading into the background. The sound so constant in her life it barely registers in her ears.

She almost wants to be able to see the scenery. Then remembers it's mile after mile of brown nothingness masked by deep night.

Music. Music would be nice. Except she lost her hard drive of tunes at Frankie's fuckpalace and turning on the radio to seek out a station is more likely to lead to the psychotic blathering of Iron Cross goons than it is The Rolling Stones.

Jefferson Airplane.

ZZ Top.

AC/DC.

Hell, she'd be happy with REO Speedwagon or Kansas right now.

Something other than the occasional sound of her leathers squeaking in the seat and Dogmeat licking himself behind her. The noise is revolting.

Athena yells at him a few times for it, then gives up.

No point.

She rolls down the window instead. Listens to the rubber on the road. Lights a cigarette.

The highway turns almost ninety degrees to the left over a long stretch.

Athena blinks. Rubs her eyes. Gets a sudden horrible feeling. Like she's falling. Disconnected from reality. Physically but not mentally. A phantom.

Her hands ain't on the wheel. Well, they *are*, but they're not. They're somewhere else. Her muscles won't listen to her. Her throat won't function. Won't swallow.

She shakes her head. Pushes her legs hard against the floor. Pushes back into her seat. Reminds her own body of where she is and tries to take control again.

Her neck twitches. Chin ticks off to the left and the right. She moves her jaw, which suddenly feels like it's gone off its runners. Her throat clicks.

Athena hits the brakes. Comes to a dead stop in the middle of the highway. Takes her sweaty hands off the steering wheel after she realizes she's been clutching it so hard they're cramped.

She puts the car in park. Shuts it off. Steps out. Drops her still-lit cigarette.

Dogmeat scrambles around her then trots off to find a suitable spot to relieve both his bladder and his bowels. Does. Then wanders along the concrete guard walls sniffing everything he can. Fuzzy butt in the Dodge's headlights.

A frown washes over Athena's face as she watches him. She knows what happened to her but she'd rather not deal with it.

Endless stress and strain and fatigue. . . .

Athena puts her hands on her knees. Bends over. "A goddamn panic attack, are you *shitting me?*" She straightens up. Runs her hands across her face. Leans back against the Hellcat. "Now I get to add my own brain to the list of assholes trying to screw this up."

She reaches in for her whiskey. Takes a mouthful. Lights a fresh cigarette.

Fishes in her pocket for one of those uppers that Mark gave her.

Comes up empty.

Ain't that perfect.

Nothing like being hunted. Having a panic attack. *And* needing a nap.

Athena mouths some more whiskey. Admits to herself that she needs rest. Looks around and can't see anything that might be suitable or safe.

She takes a deep breath. Winces. Snaps her fingers. "Dogmeat, we're outta here."

The canine growls at something in the dark. The white of his fur makes him stand out. He barks once. Snaps his jaws forward. Returns to the Hellcat in a happy prance. Tail wagging.

Athena squints at him. "Whatcha got?"

Dogmeat holds it up in the lights of the car. Not actually trying to. Just tossing his jaws around.

It's a beetle. Black with red striations. About the length and width of a deflated football. The legs spindly. Loose. A crunchy chew toy for Dogmeat that drips yellow ichor.

"Drop it," Athena says. "Can't bring that in the car."

A warble of a growl emanates from Dogmeat's throat.

Athena can imagine it being the canine version of: *But mooooooom.*

She says, "No, man. I don't want that bug jizz getting on the seats." Takes an angry step toward him. "Now."

He holds his ground for a moment. *Harumph*s. Chomps the beetle in two. Swallows what's left in his mouth as the insect's spindly legs and chunks of its carapace flop to the ground.

Athena snaps her fingers.

The dog relents. Hops into the car.

She slides behind the wheel once more. Tries to make sure her muscles know what they're doing. That her *brain* and motor functions are in the here and now.

Tells herself: *I am strong. I am death. I am the absence of forgiveness. There is no poetry for me, for I am that. Strength. Death. The absence of forgiveness.*

Mutters to herself in a croaky, faint voice: "I am strong."

Not convincing even herself.

She cracks her neck. Cranks the Hellcat's engine. Clenches and unclenches her fists. Tries to get em to stop sweating. Shaking.

Then Athena pushes on. Looks out the windows for signs of aircraft. Or pursuers. Or salvation.

There are blinks of light in the blackness high up. Planes. Choppers. Their distances and purpose wholly unknown to the Hellcat driver.

They're just that: blinks of light that move where the stars are.

A small white sign with blue text ahead tells Athena she's near some place called Winnemucca. Which is apparently "a silver star community prepared for your business."

She chuckles. "Sure." Takes exit 180. Follows a winding path of cracked asphalt between overgrown patches of bushy weeds. Cacti.

A few enormous coyotes watch the car in a disinterested way from the edges of a ranch down to her right.

Disinterested but potentially hungry.

Dogmeat stands in the backseat. Barks at the critters two or three times as big as he is.

Athena grunts. "Got a strange feeling you could take em, boy." Goes left. Crosses over I-80. Winds up in front of an RV park loaded with the skeletal remains of Winnebagos and other houses on wheels that're the size of tour buses.

Only other thing here is the charcoal remains of what might've been a front office.

She tucks the Hellcat in between the ruined recreational vehicles. A spot she doesn't think anyone's gonna be able to see from the sunken interstate a little to the north.

Athena punches the car's interior light on. Sighs. Shuts down the Hellcat. Rubs the short blonde hair on her head. She leans across the passenger seat. Works the seat forward and shoves open the door so Dogmeat can go get himself into trouble if he wants.

He doesn't, apparently. Opts to stay in the comfort of the car.

Maybe those big coyote eyes gave him something to think about.

Athena ambles to the trunk. Her body demanding nourishment more substantive than endless bottles of booze.

Why not have some stew. . . .

She shudders. Tears into the box of MREs. They ain't uniform. Not even the same manufacturer, it looks like. Just random. But who cares.

Hot macaroni and cheese sounds good to Athena.

Pasta in meat sauce for the dog.

She leans on the Hellcat while the food heats up in its pouches on the roof. Looks around. Tired. Wearier than she's ever felt before. She tries to keep her breath steady and level, but she can't.

After a few painful lungfuls of air, her knees let go and she slouches to the ground.

Without Mark's pills, all the damage her body has taken makes itself known.

Her muscles and bones scream in agony. Her fingers and joints. Her neck and her head. All the wounds that still haven't healed.

Like the memory of David. That guilt she's so good at hiding most of the time. A deeply internalized guilt that set her off on this journey.

Memories of David morph into thoughts of Mark. The terror on his face when he died—not even from the mad violence around him but the *fuckin germ* that might've still been floating around in his system.

And if it happened to him, it could happen to Michelle, too.

Or Athena.

The Hellcat driver rests her head against her precious car. The machine dusty and beaten and scarred now.

. . .Michelle. The pregnant woman who was gonna be Athena's ace in the hole when it came to gaining access to the redwoods.

So much for that.

Athena chuckles. Drinks.

Her morbid laughs become little halting sobs.

She doubts everything she's done. Every sacrifice she's made and every sacrifice she's forced others to make.

Stark terror hits her as her back heaves. "Maybe I won't get there, David." She grinds her knuckles against the blacktop she sits on. "I don't think I *can* get there, David." Skin comes away from her knuckles. Blood pools in the gaps above the bone. "What the fuck am I doing?"

Desperation and loneliness overwhelm her.

No David.

No Mark.

No Michelle.

Not even goddamn Bullhorn or Sherlock.

Just the Hellcat.

Athena takes a mouthful of whiskey. Wipes at her eyes. Lights a cigarette.

Dogmeat rounds the rear bumper of the Dodge. Sniffs in the direction of the MRE food. Sits next to Athena. Licks his chops. Waits. Then lies down next to her. His head against her thigh.

He rolls onto his back. Paws at the air. Big brown eyes searching for recognition from Athena.

She shakes her head. Licks her lips and tastes the salt from her tears. "Yeah? What?"

Dogmeat whines. Maintains his dopey pose. Paws in the air.

Athena exhales through her nose. Scratches Dogmeat behind the ears.

Which prompts him to adjust himself. Flop over again. This time with his head fully in her lap.

Athena responds by groaning. Putting her arms out. "Don't—" She sighs. Relents. Rests one hand on Dogmeat's big chest. Another on his head. "I read somewhere this kinda shit is supposed to help depression." She smirks. "Therapy dogs for—"

People who are gonna die.

For a little while, neither Athena nor Dogmeat do anything but wait there. She pets him and listens to the wind. Feels the chill in the air. Feels his soft fur and the nightmare metal under his flesh.

Till Athena catches herself dozing off.

She makes her eyes wide. Sniffs. Smacks Dogmeat's side to get the canine up. She stands and grabs her food and Dogmeat's. Dumps his MRE in the double dish with some water. Then shovels macaroni and cheese into her mouth with a big spoon.

It ain't bad.

Dogmeat seems to enjoy his too.

They finish their meals. The pooch meanders off to piss and shit as he always does. Hops in the backseat. Curls up. Buries his snout under his paws.

Athena shuts the Hellcat's doors. As much to protect the dog as keep him in at this point. She checks around the skeletons of nearby RVs. Seeks out a mostly intact toilet. Finds one that doesn't have a roof, but does have three walls.

It'll do.

She cleans up. Lights a cigarette. Chugs some whiskey. After the second mouthful, dawns on her that she doesn't really need the booze to pass out. Her default state is to be angry and drunk. Right now, she's fatigued and stressed to the point of an anxiety disorder.

Which is exactly why she keeps drinking.

Athena blows smoke. Flicks her cigarette out into the dust. Closes her door and brings the metal shutters up across all the windows. Kills the interior lights. She reclines the driver's seat all the way back. Ends up face-to-snout with Dogmeat.

She curls up and falls asleep listening to Dogmeat's breathing.

14.

Dogmeat paws Athena awake. Little whines escape his throat.

Light filters into the car through tiny slits in the metal shutters. Morning or early afternoon. She doesn't know or care which.

She sits up. Pops her seat back into place. Grabs a random bottle of water from the floor on the passenger side. There's a nasty taste in her mouth from the combination of macaroni and cheese and whiskey the night before.

So she downs some. Holds it in her cheeks. Swishes the water around in an attempt to pull some of the gross taste from her tongue and teeth.

Dogmeat whines again.

Athena makes a groan in her throat. Holds up a hand.

I'm working on it.

She slides the metal shutters down so she can spit out the window.

Goddamn Iron Cross raider is waiting on the other side of the glass. Teeth black behind a crazed smile. Eyes wide. Tattoo on his forehead and pendant around his neck.

He barks at the Hellcat driver.

More barks and howling sound off around Athena and Dogmeat.

The goon keeps his crazy eyes on her. "Wakey wakey, eggs and bakey." He smashes her window with a crowbar.

Athena spits the full load of liquid morning breath in his face. Shoves her door open so it slams into his skull. Busts his teeth and his head open.

There's a sudden sound of laughter.

Dogmeat barks. Growls. Probably wants to get outside and start biting necks like he did before at the NCR encampment.

Athena turns the engine over. Drops the other shutters so she can see what the hell is going on. . . .

The Hellcat's surrounded by Iron Cross lunatics. Two dozen or more goons who hop up and down. Play with their crotches.

Athena pulls her 1911. Hits the gas.

The car doesn't go anywhere. Its tires spin on the asphalt. Create smoke and a cringe-inducing squeal.

Athena's eye twitches. She looks in the rearview mirror.

The strange sea of asshole raider goons parts. There's a monstrosity of a truck behind her. About twenty feet away. Some heavy-hauling eighteen-wheeler. A semi like a Peterbilt or a Mack that's engulfed by slabs of metal armor. Almost looks like a train where the entire front is an oversized cowcatcher. The cab is open. A big cage with thick bars. Spikes. Barbed wire. Speakers on the top and the sides.

She sees a chain leading from the back of the Hellcat to a winch at the front of the truck.

Also sees the big sonuvabitch behind the wheel. He stands.

Some insane bald bastard rocking S&M gear. A chain that links his pierced nipples through holes cut into a black leather vest. Black chaps with the freak's studded banana hammock exposed.

The Western Devil.

He lifts a microphone to his mouth. His voice is blasted into the air by all the speakers on his big rig. "Oh, Hellbitch. I've been waiting for this."

Athena grunts. Considers her options.

None of em good.

Athena's knuckles crack as her grip tightens on the steering wheel.

She shakes her head. "I've come too goddamn far. Too goddamn far." She keeps the Hellcat's engine running. Clicks the walkie-talkie's transmission button. Says on the NCR's channel. "If you fuckers have any intention of showing up, now's a good time." She takes a chance. Steps out. Snaps at Dogmeat so that he stays in. Glares at all the Iron Cross around her.

If the rotten pricks had simply wanted her dead—or the Hellcat destroyed—they coulda done that a hundred times by now. And yet, she's still kicking.

The Devil probably wants to toy with her. Threaten her with varying forms of sexual molestation.

Which buys her time.

Time she needs.

Athena keeps the walkie-talkie on her chest. Grenade launcher slung over her shoulder. But she doesn't let her hands go anywhere near the 1911 at her side.

She cocks an eye at the Devil. "Fuck do you want?"

The Devil fiddles with the chains that link his nipples and his studded banana hammock. "I want you, of course."

"Why? Cuz I murdered so many of your little fuckboys here?" She juts her chin at the surrounding goons. "They really ain't all that good at, well, anything at all."

The Devil bounces his head from side to side. "*Wellllll.*" He tugs at his banana hammock. "You can save the attitude, kitten. You've been such a pain in the ass that I've got a stiff cockrocket just keeping you trapped here."

Athena grunts. Tries to figure out what the fuck she's gonna do. Keeps the Devil talking. "What're we doing here, Mr. Devil?" She spreads her hands. "You wanted me. You got me."

The Devil chuckles. "Do I though? See—" He holds up his hands. Wiggles his fingers in the air as though he's playing an invisible piano at high speeds. "I think when I've 'got you,' you'll be begging to join the Iron Kennel. You'll *want* to be the vessel for my future soldiers."

Athena's eyes dart around. Still ain't any good options. But she thinks she can get a grenade off. Not at the Devil—that semi's too close for the explosive to arm—but one of the other vehicles. Make one of their hideous skull trucks go boom. Pull the 1911. Shoot the winch to free the Dodge. Drive like hell. Except there's no way a .45 is gonna snap steel.

So, actually, she's boned.

The Devil points at her. "No, I don't think so, kitten."

The raider she clocked in the head with the car door rams her in the gut with the butt of his rifle.

She doubles over. Coughs. Vomits.

He grabs the strap of her grenade launcher. Cuts it in two with a razor sharp knife. He hisses in her ear. Bleeds on her while he talks. "I told you we were gonna get you, Hellbitch."

Dogmeat barks and paces inside the car. He snarls. Pushes his face against the windows. Smears em with spittle and foam.

Athena growls. Fights to catch her breath.

When the raider stands and taps the car windows to antagonize Dogmeat, she bolts upright. Locks her hands around his neck. Slams her robotic right knee into his balls. Once. Twice. Knees him in the gut. Lets go and bangs his head against the Hellcat.

His eyes twirl in their sockets. He slumps to the ground.

The crowd of Iron Cross laughs. Hoots.

She pulls her 1911. Puts a .45 slug in his face. Snaps her aim to target the Devil. Manages to squeeze a shot off. The bullet bounces off the bars of the cage on the Devil's rig.

He doesn't flinch.

Just stares.

Then he laughs too.

This huge baritone mockery that spews from the semi's speakers.

Before she can pull the trigger again, she's bum rushed by three other goons. They tackle her with enough force to bounce her off the Dodge. Rock it hard enough to make it wobble on its suspension.

They pin her against the asphalt. Kick her sides. One holds a boot to her neck. They all grin and chuckle. *Heh heh. Stupid cow. Stupid blonde bitch.* They remove her weapons.

Strip her of her 1911. Her shotgun. Her magazines and ammo. Toss em away.

They flip her over. Search her with brutish, invasive hands and fingers that slither along her breasts. Between her thighs.

One peels her leather jacket off while the other two hold her legs. Her hands. Her throat.

The NCR walkie-talkie skitters away on the asphalt. Still on. Still receiving.

The Devil says, "Like any wild animal, kitten, you need to be broken down and broken in so that you can be a. . .*productive* member of the team." He gestures to the circus of raiders. "Because, when I look around here, I see team players." He winks. "The drugs help, of course."

Iron Cross goons whoop it up and cheer.

The three holding Athena stand her up. Hands forced behind her back.

She sneers. "So you think you're gonna make me a good submissive girl? For what? Babies? Ain't gonna happen. The tech in my leg from Frankie? Whatever it is, you oughtta get a move on. I'm past my prime and pretty fuckin close to the expiration date."

The Devil makes a *tsk tsk tsk* noise. "Part of that is true. I think that *you* will be my greatest prize. My trophy." His free hand glides along his chest. Down to his cock. He frees it from the studded banana hammock. Plays with himself and moans. "*Mmm.* I can see you in the Iron Kennel. Then I'll spread you out and attach you to the front of my rig like a hood ornament. That pale ass jiggling on the road. Staring at your pussy as it bounces around."

He stops. Grins. Dick hard as a hammer. "*That* part is true. But I don't need any of the technology I *might* be able to reverse engineer from your leg. Already got access to Frankie's files. And they have been *very* inspirational." He tugs on another smaller chain that leads to somewhere behind the caged cab of the truck.

A naked and beaten young black man stumbles forward so he's shoulder to shoulder with the Devil. Collar around his neck.

Long gashes that are fat with pus and congealed blood mar his chest. His skin suffers from massive patches of purple.

There's a spiked ball-gag in his mouth. Some of the points poke against the flesh of his cheeks. Others have pushed through the skin in a ring around his crimson-leaking lips.

The man's eyes are frenzied. Endlessly weeping.

They meet Athena's.

The Hellcat driver frowns. Whispers. "Sherlock. . . ."

The Devil tugs on the spiked ball gag with a gloved hand.

Fresh blood dribbles from Sherlock's mouth. His cries of pain are muffled.

"When you all escaped Frankie's, I guess you didn't notice that my young charge here slipped away with a hard drive just *pregnant* with data." The Devil giggles. Then he's shrieking. Insane. "But *he* had some goofy *goddamn idea* about using it to research a cure." Another giggle. "He didn't want to give it to me." The Devil licks his lips. Looks to Athena. "We've done great things with Frankie's goodies."

Athena snarls. "I got a hard time believing your dumbfuck goons can even *read*, forget about understanding Frankie's technology."

"Kitten, I hope I didn't overestimate you. You can't possibly be that stupid." He smirks at her. "The Iron Cross is vast. My goons have *their* job. As do my builders and my brainiacs. They make excellent use of our space at Edwards Air Force Base, which is ours. As is Groom Lake." He grins. "Which most folks knew as Area 51."

Athena doesn't have anything to say to that. She just stares.

The Devil says, "There's all kinds of fun shit in there, kitten." He rubs his chest. "Now—" He nods to the goons.

They pull Athena away from the Hellcat and the barking Dogmeat inside.

Athena kicks. Roars.

Goons respond by punching her in the stomach again. Knocking the wind outta her.

The sound of a new engine joins the fray. A diesel beast. A fat yellow bulldozer. Its treads rumble over the remains of the RV park office. Plow through the dusty bones of a trailer. The blade in front lifted a few feet off the ground.

Psychotic raiders cheer at the sight.

Athena struggles against the Iron Cross holding her.

The bulldozer comes to a rocky stop just in front of the Hellcat.

Athena screams. Fights. Kicks and tries to bite the raiders.

Dogmeat jumps from side to side in the back seat. Barks and barks. He locks his eyes on Athena. Howls until he has no breath. Howls again.

The Devil croons into the microphone: "I. . .Fall. . .To pieces. . . ."

The bulldozer blade comes crashing down onto the Hellcat's hood. Metal there crumples. Pinches in. The front of the Dodge pitches forward. Hits the asphalt. The back jumps into the air.

Dogmeat is thrown forward. Poor dog can't do a damn thing about it.

Neither can Athena.

She screams. Roars. Her face burns red. Her heart punches against her ribs. Her blood boils in her veins. "Fuck you. *Fuck you.*"

The Devil laughs. Sticks his tongue out. Licks the air.

The bulldozer blade comes down again.

Pops the front tires.

The sound of the air exploding is a pitiful yelp of pain and sadness to Athena's ears.

A goon grabs her by the hair at the back of her head. Another hoots in front of her. Spits in her face. Rubs his greasy cheeks against her breasts then delivers a brutal knee to her gut.

She doubles over. The raiders let her fall.

One stomps a boot on the small of her back.

Another drags her by her hair and forces her chin up to watch as the bulldozer continues is sadistic attack on the Hellcat.

Tears well in Athena's eyes. Tumble in rivulets. The clear mixes with the red under her face.

She closes her eyes. Gasps. Blinks. Looks from side to side in a desperate attempt to find some way to fight back.

The NCR walkie-talkie is right next to her.

She strains her ears to listen.

Voices. There are *voices*.

Athena holds her breath.

The bulldozer blade slams into the Hellcat's engine.

Her precious machine's precious heart.

Dogmeat barks in a fury that nears complete hysteria.

There's a crack of thunder high above.

It catches the attention of the raiders with a powerful suddenness. They stop. The laughter and hoots die down. They look up and around. Try to find the source.

The Devil shouts into his microphone. Commands his troops. "Go. *Go now.* Unhook the winch. Move the motherfucking trucks, it's the—"

An explosion tears through the ranks of the Iron Cross. Sends bodies and limbs flying. Meaty chunks of dickheads splatter against their comrades and their vehicles. Gore rains as though someone was throwing tomato soup around.

The shockwave hammers Athena's eardrums. She feels the pressure in her head. Her innards. She wasn't even that close.

It blows out the remaining windows on the Hellcat. Causes Dogmeat to flop down between the seats.

It knocks away the goons holding her.

Forces em to cover their faces and their eyes.

Athena bolts upright. Grabs the nearest goon. Headbutts him. She yanks the knife on his belt free. Stabs him in the stomach. Pulls the blade out. Shoves it again and again and again into his face until it looks like it's been through a deli slicer.

The Devil's big rig blows its horn. It turns tail. Hauls ass down the road. A few trucks attempt to follow.

Three attack choppers scream by. Laser beams of bullets rip apart the cab of the bulldozer. The driver inside explodes. A bucket of red paint.

Screaming raiders who raise their rifles and attempt to shoot the helicopters down are reduced to tiny giblets by high caliber rounds.

Athena scrambles for her 1911. Checks the mag. Finds the second asshole who was holding her. Rushes him. Rams him in the spine with a lowered shoulder.

He tumbles. Lands with an *"Urk."*

Athena shoots him three times in the back of the head. Shatters his skull with .45 bullets. Finds the third motherfucker. Puts a round through each of his knees.

The raider falls to the ground. Squeals about his legs.

Athena drops her empty mag. Doesn't have a fresh one handy. Holsters her 1911. Runs to the fallen goon.

He holds his hands up. "No *no no*."

Athena brings her right boot heel down on his jaw. Cracks it in half. Stomps again and shoves the bones into the meat of his brain.

She roadie runs to the Hellcat. Falls to her knees at the driver's side door. A muted sob gets stuck in her throat. She furrows her brow. Plays her fingers over the car's exterior. Blood cuts paths through the dust.

"I'm sorry."

Athena grips the door handle. Throws it open.

Dogmeat leaps out. Lips upturned in a snarl.

Athena locks her hands around his neck. Barks. "Kill every fuckin one of em."

Dogmeat barks back. Bolts off. A creature built for speed.

She's never seen him run. It's amazing.

He gallops. Sees an asshole he wants and takes off. A race car among canines. He jumps. Lands on a raider's back. The guy drops and screams for a moment.

Till Dogmeat embeds his teeth in the guy's neck. Shakes. Pulls away sinew and tissue. Chews some of the meat and digs in again. His white and peach-colored fur is stained red quick.

Athena grunts. Briefly searches the battered Hellcat for spare 1911 mags. Gives up. Crawls toward her sawed-off shotgun. Her jacket. Snatches up both.

A goon tackles her as she throws her leather over her shoulders. She lands on her back.

He straddles her. Wraps two hands around her neck. "You can't defy him forever. He's going to make the things Frankie created look like *toys*."

Athena strains to keep breathing. A low noise rumbles in her throat. She reaches into her left holster. Grips the shotgun handle. Tilts it up. "Uh huh." Pulls both triggers.

Pellets burst the raider's side. A torrent of blood streams from him. Coats Athena in warm stickiness.

He screeches.

She pounds the hot shotgun barrels against his Adam's Apple. Downs the sonuvabitch for good. Breaks open the sawed-off. Searches for more shells in her pockets but doesn't find any.

Athena tucks the scattergun into its home on her left side. Empty like the 1911. She ducks as the attack choppers make another run.

Their cannons make short work of another line of raiders.

The rotten shitburgers jiggle. Dance. Their skin and skeletons pop under the onslaught of precisely-directed murder.

Ain't much left of the Iron Cross.

Ain't much left of the Hellcat.

She looks up. Watches the gunships peel away. Head back west. The massive AC-130 attack plane that brought the initial burst of thunder way, way up there makes a slow circle then follows the path of the choppers.

Athena sighs. Leans against the Hellcat. Digs in her jacket. Finds a single unbroken cigarette in the pack among all its little broken brothers. She lights it. Straightens up. Watches Dogmeat chew on another struggling Iron Cross goon's neck.

Last one, far as she can tell.

The dog laps up some of the blood. Some of the meat.

His ears go up when he locks eyes with her again. His party hats.

He trots over. Tail wagging. He sits in front of her. Fur no longer anything near white.

His face is an expression she translates as: *Hey, ya see what I did? I did a good job, huh? Okay. Great! We agree. I now require petting and treats.*

Athena smirks. "Least one of us is having a good time." Her hand moves from scratching Dogmeat to the Hellcat.

She turns. Rests her arms on the roof of her machine. Lays her chin there. Takes a deep breath. Winces. Lets her skin stay on the metal. Turns her cheek so it's flat there.

Sobs.

Her left hand caresses the windshield. Her right stretches over the roof.

She wipes her eyes. Listens as a plane touches down behind her. Its wheels *chuff* when they touch the dirt outside of town. Then roll as they near Athena's nightmare on the asphalt.

The ass of a big C-130J opens up. Ramp comes down.

Athena turns away from the Hellcat. Watches NCR troopers funnel out. Take up position with a combination of light machine guns and carbines.

Oliver walks down the ramp. Between the line of New California Republic soldiers. He sees Athena. Steadies himself. Marches toward her.

Dogmeat waits at her side. Whining.

Athena says, "Good timing, dipshit. A little sooner and. . . ." She stops. "My *Hellcat* would still be alive." She squints at him. "You *let the Hellcat die.*"

The small army of NCR troopers watch her warily.

Oliver shakes his head. "We had two options: Keep trying to wake you up or save an uncontaminated pregnant woman." He shrugs. "Ben and I, we threw some shit near the trunk of your car to keep you going."

Athena nods. Lips curled down. "Yeah." She mouths whiskey. Smokes.

Oliver says, "You wanna kill these motherfuckers? You wanna make the world *better* in the wake of this, where some asshole has delusions of grandeur? Of being Frankie Number Two?"

Athena rolls her tongue around in her mouth. Looks to Dogmeat.

The pooch stained red.

He's suddenly voiceless. Can't be bothered to whine or growl.

She looks at her own fucked up hands and the blood all over her body.

Finally, she nods.

15.

Athena doesn't feel like she has a choice. And she's exhausted. Beat to shit. She'd enjoy a shower. A nap.

She sits in the cargo bay of Oliver's plane. Some thousands of feet over the tired dead desert of America's western coast.

"Too much weight," Oliver says over the din of the engines. "We're loaded for war. Haven't been that way in a while, but now every C-130 and AC-130 gunship either carries enough to supply an army or enough to wipe one out."

Only got room and weight enough for Athena and Dogmeat. No Hellcat.

Oliver says: "This is it. We all. . . ." He stops. Shrugs. "NCR is in war mode. We gotta go on the offensive after the attack on Salt Lake. So. . .Extra weight is for supplies not. . . ." He looks to Athena. "Not dead cars." Pause. "I'm sorry."

Athena grunts. Waves for Dogmeat to plant his fuzzy head in her lap.

He does so happily.

She says, "Yeah." Pets her pooch.

Oliver says, "Look. I've tried to be straight with you."

Athena bobs her head.

Oliver runs a hand over his face. Clearly a bit frazzled. Frustrated. "We're flying into Reno for resupply. Then we're going to Beale."

Athena scratches her chin. Remembers the badge and the star from the satchel. "Beale is *your* home base. . .Gonna guess it's an air force base." She nods. "Western Devil says they've got Edwards and Area 51."

"We know." Oliver plants his ass by hers and Dogmeat's on a nearby seat.

She tries to find the words. Can't. "I feeling kinda lost here, Oliver. You said you'd take me to California. That still on the table?"

Oliver sighs. "Yeah. But I'd say it's been pushed a little farther back on that figurative table."

Athena squints. Stares at her feet. "I'm tired. I'm real, real tired."

Oliver takes a deep breath. "I know, Athena."

She bristles when he says her name instead of the nom de guerre she's used to.

Hellcat.

The machine she left behind.

Yet here's her leg. And here's Dogmeat.

Two machines. She ain't sure how much they're worth right now, though.

Oliver fidgets in his seat. Makes like he's gonna put a hand on her shoulder. Try to offer some comfort. He retreats from the motion a moment later. Maybe thinks better. Maybe worries Athena's gonna tear his damn head off if he touches her.

She wouldn't.

Not right now, anyway.

"I'm tired, Oliver." She frowns and looks at him. Scratches the side of her head. "I'm *tired*."

Oliver looks to Athena.

Then Dogmeat. The canine still stained with gore.

Wouldn't wanna be on the wrong end of those jaws.

Oliver says, "What do you want me to do?"

"Take me to bed." Athena frowns.

Oliver nods. Furrows his brow. Holds out his hand.

Athena takes it. Allows him to help her stand. "They killed the Hellcat, Oliver."

"I know, Athena." He guides her through the C-130J's cargo hold. Up through the barracks. The medical area where Michelle used to be but ain't anymore.

He takes her to a tiny room set off to the side. The door swings in and he shows her where commanding officers can get some sleep on a double mattress. The pillows are scarce but the thermal blankets are plentiful.

Athena crawls away from Oliver's grasp. Buries herself under the blankets. Digs in like a tick.

Dogmeat growls at Oliver. Doesn't seem to like the fact that the military man is between him and Athena.

Athena barks at the dog. "Stop. *Stop*."

Dogmeat whines.

She looks to Oliver.

His face is still one of concern. Eyebrows arched.

She reaches out. Grabs Oliver's hand. Pulls him down onto the bed.

Dogmeat growls anew.

Athena shouts: "*Relax.*"

She kicks the door shut.

Intertwines Oliver's fingers with her own.

The lone light above them in the cubby hums.

Athena shifts under the blankets. Wraps herself up in a fetal position. Squeezes Oliver's hand. Pulls air in and out through her nose.

Oliver watches her. Tries to smile.

There are no words between the two. Just eye contact held for minute after minute.

Athena feels herself falling asleep. Her body cries out for relief. Her mind cries for an end to the nightmare.

The end of the road.

Oliver doesn't let go of her hand. He uses his free one to grip her shoulder. Gives it a gentle squeeze that lingers as her eyelids flutter.

Athena closes her eyes.

Reality begins to fade away.

She says without thinking, "Thank you, David."

16.

It ain't much sleep, but it's the first real *rest* she's gotten since she left New York. That night at the Dapper Brothers' radio station comes close. Except she was so fucked up on booze and regret she couldn't appreciate it.

She feels. . .better when she opens the door. Sees Dogmeat waiting for her.

He wags his tail at the sight of her. Stands. Rears back and tries to land his paws on her chest.

Which makes Athena jump back. "No, no. I don't need a hundred pounds of dog landing on my messed up body right now, okay?" She pats his side and he leans on her.

She makes her way toward the front of the plane. The cockpit.

Oliver cranes his neck from the pilot seat. Gives her a curt nod. Talks into his headset at the air traffic controller on the ground. "Yeah, roger that Reno. Headshed wants all the birds back in the air. So just refit and refuel and then kick those troopers out."

The city is laid out in front of em. A sprawl of old casinos and dusty golf courses and densely packed residential housing. All flat and squat.

Unlike Salt Lake, seems as though the New California Republic has a real presence here. A population that exists beyond the meager confines of an airport. There are people in the streets. Ant-sized from this height, but they're still there. Including foot patrols that march across the massive golf courses. APCs and tanks and jeeps that rolls through different sections of the city.

For a moment, Athena feels something like hope.

Hope that the NCR is doing the right thing.

Hope that they're the good guys and she hasn't made the wrong choice.

Again.

Then there's a flash.

Then there's a small mushroom cloud rising on the far side of Reno.

And another.

Oliver's female copilot gasps. "Oh my God." She moans. Makes a pitiful noise. "*No.*"

"Get everyone in the goddamn air right *now*, Reno," Oliver shouts into his mic. Just before throwing his headset across the room with rage.

He pulls back on the stick. Brings the C-130J's nose up at a sudden severe pitch that makes Athena grasp for something to hold onto and sends Dogmeat tumbling. The plane dips left as the NCR sergeant sets it on a new course.

The aircraft levels out.

Athena watches the mushroom clouds float up higher in the air. Begin to dissipate.

The female NCR pilot does the same. Finally says, "We should. . . ." Her voice trails off into nothingness.

Athena knows what the woman was gonna say.

She was gonna say that they should assist their trooper comrades. Land and join the fight. Except the idea's crazy.

You might wanna do the right thing, but you don't fly *into* nuclear explosions.

More planes and choppers join Oliver's C-130J in the air. So at least some other folks made it out.

But combat on the ground has to be utter chaos.

Even if you're a badass part of a badass team of troopers, the idea of nuclear suicide bombers is fuckin scary.

Oliver's voice is slow and sad. "Know what's completely goddamn insane about this?" He doesn't seem to be talking to anyone in particular, so nobody says anything back. He continues: "We're *lucky*. We're lucky the rotten scum of the Iron Cross can't get more material together to make anything bigger than a few dirty bombs."

Which doesn't mean there are any fewer troopers dead.

He says, "If we wanted to, *we* could nuke the bastards into oblivion. But we fuckin *don't*. Why? Because *we* actually wanna rebuild this country and we don't wanna turn it into more of an irradiated fuckin wasteland than it already is."

Athena walks forward against the incline of the plane. She stops when she gets to Oliver's side. Hesitates. Then holds his shoulder. Says, "What's the plan?"

Oliver grunts. "We're gonna head to Beale. Gear up." He locks eyes with Athena. "Then we're gonna stomp these motherfuckers." He turns back to the controls. Squints out the windows. Talks to Athena without making eye contact. "You still have the badge and the star we left for you?"

"Yeah. Why?" Athena mulls the word "we" and says, "Where *is* Ben? I mean, Corporal Whitmore. . .Or however the fuck you're supposed to address people."

"Ben's at Beale with the generals. The headshed. He's got as much field experience—maybe more—as anyone in the NCR. Including the brass. They're working on an attack strategy."

"Wait so. . .you flew out here on your own to get me?" Athena feels her stomach drop. A little happiness in her mind. A little smile crosses her lips.

"Well—" Oliver glances at her. "Not alone, but it was my operation, yeah." He clears his throat. "Anyway, again, get that star and badge on. Folks who ain't NCR don't get to go where we're going now."

"What're they gonna do? Bitch at me till I find my hall pass?"

"No. They'll shoot you."

Athena grunts. "If this is your magical safe place, and I'm a pawn, can you at least tell me where the fuck Michelle is? The pregnant woman."

Oliver nods. Mouth a frown. "We flew her to New Eden. The redwoods. That's why it took a while to get back to you."

Athena grunts again.

Realizes in that instant her selfish plan is now utterly fucked.

* * *

The plane comes in low over a wild expanse of lush forest. Athena doesn't remember ever seeing so much green. All the trees that reach over one another along the hills to gobble sunlight.

Farther out are long stretches of grass. Fields. Occasionally pockmarked by ponds or small lakes. Creeks and streams cut their own winding path through the terrain.

It's beautiful.

At the base itself is every manner of flying or rolling murder. A handful of jets. Dozens of attack choppers of varying design. More AC-130 gunships. Tanks whose names Athena does not know. Armored personnel carriers. Humvees. There are even big guns. Artillery pieces.

All those death-dealers surrounded by an overabundance of nature.

Oliver's plane touches down. The wheels squeak. They roll along the tarmac. Slow next to a bunch of small winged craft without cockpits.

Drones, Athena figures.

Oliver kills the engines. Stands. Pats Athena's shoulder as he marches back toward the cargo bay. Even gives Dogmeat a quick scratch. Then pushes on and lowers the ramp for his soldiers to disembark.

Athena joins him with Dogmeat.

He raises his eyebrows. Nods to her once. Heads outside.

Athena looks to Dogmeat. Cocks an eye.

He whines.

She says, "Yeah, all right."

There are four stiffs outside waiting. Two men and two women. Different ages. Different races. Their sandy uniforms are significantly more prim and proper than any other NCR soldier's. Shoes shiny. Clothes clean.

The generals.

With stars along their shoulders.

They stand upright. Hands behind their backs. Chests out. Chins high.

Athena doesn't like any of it. She with her worn and torn black road leathers. 1911 on her right. Shotgun on her left. Blood everywhere. Cigarette between her lips. Whiskey forever on her breath.

The generals eyeball her as she walks down the ramp. Apparently feeling the same way she does.

Like, *Who's this asshole?*

One of the women speaks. "This's her?"

Oliver stands off to the side. Away from em a little bit. He nods even though nobody's watching except Athena. "This is the Hellcat."

"She looks like road runner trash."

Athena cocks an eye. Smokes. She lifts the right leg of her leather trousers. Shows off the chrome. "Shiny trash."

The generals grumble.

Oliver says, "We need her to move forward."

"Well," says one of the male generals. "We need her leg."

Athena sucks in her cheeks. "You dipshits know the Western Devil already has Frankie's tech, right? Has access to the data from Frankie's computers? If you think suicide nukers and big bugs were bad, just give em another month. Or, hell, a week."

One of the generals says, "And how do you know that?"

Athena smirks. "The Devil told me." Smokes. "You wanna get ahead of the game, you talk to me."

The generals grumble.

Then one bleats. "Holy shit, a dog."

Dogmeat trots down the ramp. His ears go up. *Aroo?*

The generals spend the next five minutes fawning over Dogmeat. Petting him. Giving him belly rubs while he lies there and soaks up attention.

Till one finds the hole in his hide. Looks to Athena. "He's—"

Athena nods. "Yeah. Another Frankie refugee." Athena tilts her head. "What happens now?"

A female general steps away from Dogmeat. "If you're going to be a part of the NCR, then you're going to fight alongside the NCR. Everyone fights."

"What do I need to do?"

"Go inside. Get geared up." The woman goes back to playing with Dogmeat.

"Wait, wait." Athena holds up a hand. "*Heyoo.*" She claps her hands together. "I'm not. . . ." She shrugs. "I don't work the frontlines. I can't be an effective trooper for you. I've never been a soldier and I don't take orders well."

"We know." She looks up from Dogmeat's fur. "That's why you're going in with Master Sergeant Bradley for an insertion."

"Insertion *where.*"

"The heart of the Iron Cross." The general grins. "Area 51."

* * *

Athena stares at the walls of the armory after getting cleaned up. The place is massive. Two stories of concrete and metal walls. Metal shelves and weapon racks. Fluorescent lights buzz overhead.

The guns go on for. . .forever. She locates mags that'll play nice with her Springfield Armory 1911. Tucks those, loaded, into her gun and three spares into a low-slung holster on her thigh.

The sawed-off in her left holster is easy to feed. She grabs shells. Stuffs em into her jacket pockets.

When it comes to a primary, she's less sure.

Oliver appears beside her. "You thinking about close quarters?"

Athena nods.

Oliver says, "You familiar at all with assault rifles?"

Athena shakes her head. "Assault rifles are a different beast from what I'm used to."

He points. Says, "The M4 is a mainstay for a reason. And the Famas gets good marks all around. There's the Tavor TAR-21—"

Athena grunts. "This is all 5.56 shit though, right? I want something that puts cantaloupe-sized holes in these fuckers."

"For CQB."

"*Yes.*"

Oliver grins. "You want .45-caliber hell?" Walks a little farther down the armory. Produces a key from a chain around his neck. Opens a long metal drawer. Gestures for her to come closer.

Athena does. Smiles when she sees what's inside.

Several Thompson submachine guns. The gun that won World War II. They're relics, but they appear to be flawless. Pristine.

She plucks one up. Feels the weight. Tucks the wooden stock against her shoulder. "How many mags?"

Oliver sucks his teeth. "Mix. Few sticks and a few drums."

"Gimme all of em."

* * *

An hour later, everyone's standing in front of the generals. Big assembly Athena has no interest in. She *hears* more than she *listens*—and she's only hearing on account of there's nothing else to fill her ears.

"We aren't fighting merely to protect our lives. But to protect the lives of the children who will inherit this land after us. These battles today, they tell the raiders that we will *not* submit. We will *not* lie down while they rape an already wounded world."

Athena makes little talking-hand gestures to herself as she secures her gear at the rear of Oliver's C-130J. "Wom wom. . .womwomwom."

There's a rapturous applause.

A minute while the troopers run to where they're supposed to be.

Then Oliver is at her side again.

He pats her shoulder and charges into his C-130J. Starts the engines.

Dogmeat barks.

Athena shakes her head. "You gotta stay here on this one, pal."

Bark.

"Yeah, I'll forgive you if you make friends with other humans."

Whine.

She takes his long head into her hands. "You'll be all right." Scratches him behind the ears. Then stands and points away from the ramp. "Get along, motherfucker."

Dogmeat barks.

The ramp Athena's on starts to close.

She mutters, "Gonna be a fun ride."

17.

Evening takes over the sky. Light fades alongside the frames of a hundred aircraft.

Gunships. Troop transports.

They peel away while Oliver's C-130J heads southeast to Area-51.

Athena's never seen so many vehicles. Murderous intent or not. She simply hasn't. Helicopters and planes drop away from her path. Begin to bombard areas either held by the Iron Cross or suspected as such.

Missiles streak.

The guns are fireworks.

Athena feels Oliver's plane begin its descent.

The troops in the cargo hold with Athena pump their chests and their fists.

This is their job. And she figures they're probably very good at it.

She hears the thunder of AC-130 gunships to their left at right pound the area with fire and death.

Oliver appears in the entranceway that separates the cargo hold from the rest of the plane. He shouts. "Plane ain't gonna stop. We're gonna drag the ramp. You get the fuck off fast as you can. Find cover behind the concrete blocks that litter the runway. And you kill anything that moves."

The troops watch him. Salute. "Yes, sir."

"You with me?" His eyes move to Athena's.

NCR soldiers yell. "We're with you."

Oliver's eyes don't leave Athena's. "I said, *are you with me?*"

Athena shouts with the congregation. "We're with you." She checks the drum mag on her Thompson submachine gun. Kisses it.

Oliver hops down the stairs. Tucks his M4 carbine against his chest. Nods. "Let's go." He circles a hand around his head.

The ramp descends.

The plane hits the runway.

Troopers throw themselves out and roll against inertia two by two.

Oliver grabs the lapel of Athena's jacket. Looks her square in the eye.

They jump together. Roll.

She finds herself on an asphalt airstrip about forty feet from the front of an aircraft hangar and a bunker entrance. Scuttles to find cover behind a concrete block.

One of those mad titan bugs lurches around at the far end the tarmac. Jets roar toward it. Rockets drop from their wings. Zoom toward their target.

Oliver is near. M4 in his hands. He takes shots at the raiders who run in a panic to set up defensive positions. Short bursts that punch into the flesh of his targets.

Athena does the same. Pops up from cover with the Thompson tucked to her shoulder. Lays down a hail of fire with .45 slugs that chew bloody holes in the raiders.

Tanks in the dusty fields behind Athena pound the airport structures with shells. The enormous rounds make holes in the stone and metal of the Iron Cross. Helicopters bring their own kind of support. Cannons and miniguns that turn raiders into smears on the airstrip.

Athena has a moment to think: *This is all so pretty in the purple and orange light of the evening.* Then: *Holy piss, it's so loud.*

Oliver shouts at her over the din. "Main bunker. *Now.* Move up."

Athena keeps her head down. "Where the fuck—" Bullets whiz by the concrete block she's tucked behind. Explosions tear men and women apart. Most are raiders. A few are NCR troopers.

She'd like to avoid the same fate.

She screams. "Where? *Where* the fuck am I running to?"

Oliver points at a concrete doorway with a rusty metal door forty feet from the both of em. "Get goddamn *there.*"

Athena sneers. Looks over the concrete block. Sees a team of four NCR troopers planting charges. Looks up. Sees a flurry of attack choppers streak overhead.

Somewhere high above, an AC-130 is firing its cannons. Making thunder. Creating explosions that ruin the lives of anyone caught in the eruptions of fire.

Athena considers yelling at Oliver again. Doesn't.

What good would it do.

She curls around the concrete block. Runs low. Clotheslines a raider who's about to open up on Oliver's position. Fills his chest with a dose of .45 rounds that split his rib cage and make the bones bloom up amid a cascade of gore. Continues on. Throws herself against the side of the bunker doors where a team of NCR troopers are ready to blow it to pieces.

One of em hollers "Clear!" Blows the doors with an explosion and a rolling cloud of debris.

Athena grunts. Shakes her head. Blinks. Tries to make sure she ain't suddenly deaf. She throws herself through the smoke. Keeps the Thompson up. Hates this idea that she's a soldier who's supposed to work as part of a team.

Cuz fuck that.

But she does anyway.

The entrance to the bunker is a long concrete ramp that's angled down. There aren't any of the bluish fluorescent lights. Instead, it's all old yellow incandescent bulbs hidden behind little metal grates.

Athena shouts, "Clear." Her boots clomp against the concrete floor. Down. She inches up to a corner in the hall. Peeks around. Tommy gun up. If The Western Devil wants to be Frankie II then he might have all kinds of goofy shit running around.

A team of NCR troopers follows Athena in then holds position behind Athena.

As does Oliver.

He taps her shoulder. "What'd you see when you were at Frankie's?"

She rounds the corner. Another dim hallway awaits. This as one as wide as a highway, but empty. She says, "Why?"

"If he wants to do the same thing as Frankie, it might give us an edge to know what's coming."

Athena shrugs in the puke-shaded light. "Just. . .A lot of fucked up monster stuff. Ain't any way to know for sure."

"What about Frankie himself?"

"He was basically a bitch when we found him. Little scrawny fruitcake."

One of the troopers shouts. "Incoming." The others fan out to cover the wide stretch of concrete.

The hall ahead is flooded with shadows that dance across the walls. The silhouettes of bodies. Arms and legs. Shrieks of "Help me. *Help me*."

Athena tightens her grip on the Thompson. "Don't fuckin listen to em."

Another trooper says, "Why not?"

"I've fought Frankie. The Devil wants to be Frankie? The Devil's gonna throw all his little gremlins our way."

They come.

Oh, they come.

A swarm of half-formed men, women and children. Pink. With skin that hangs the same way rags do on a holocaust victim. They're all eyes and teeth. Both bulge from what a normal human might call their natural place.

The other troopers hesitate.

Athena doesn't.

She pulls the trigger on her Thompson. Sends .45 rounds into the bodies and faces of the malformed things that stream through the hallway.

Quick bursts aimed at their heads to put em down.

A few get through.

They scream "Help me, *help me*" at skittish NCR soldiers who can't put a sick dog to rest.

When the malformed, drooping things get to em. They slap their sloping skin around the paralytic troopers.

And that melting flesh melts the troopers.

A wretched child-thing locks itself around the torso of a New California Republic soldier.

The soldier can't seem to bring herself to kill a kid.

The kid screeches. "Help me."

The kid's flesh digs itself into the soldier's. Takes it over. Like one chunk of Silly Putty meeting another.

They become a rancid, hissing amalgamation of flesh.

Other troopers keep their distance.

Oliver shouts for a flamethrower unit.

Athena grunts. Turns her gun on the abomination. Her bullets punch holes in their bodies. Canyons that are quickly filled by blood and pus. Craters in meat. When the slugs hit their heads, they topple in a heap. Two figures interlinked by parasitic skin.

She doesn't care that she just ganked a kid and a comrade. Drops the empty drum mag for the Thompson and locks a fresh one in its place.

She barks, "Hear me when I say: shit gets fucked. Doesn't matter who you are." She walks slow. Not a crouch quite, but low. Farther into the bunker. Concrete and those puke-yellow lights all around. "The cure for these assholes is always the same."

The hall leads down again.

Pipes become prevalent. They're embedded in the concrete and give off a lotta heat.

The bunker turns into a sauna.

With every step, the temperature rises.

And fifty feet down, the architecture starts to change. Concrete walls give way to tapestries of skin pinned to the wall with pikes and nail guns. Some of the skin is pale. Some is tan. Some came from a hairy asshole. Some came from literal assholes.

Athena wrinkles her nose.

She doesn't know what a fan of Frankie might do. Might create. Some bizarre copycat of the craziest person she's ever even heard of. The lunatic wannabe of a lunatic wannabe.

The leaky acid-skin kids were new. But what else?

Athena cocks an eye. Minds her corners as the hallway opens up again. Gets wider and wider. Gives way to an auditorium space.

She sees a raider on guard. Two. Offers both bursts from the Thompson. Bullets make their skin erupt. Little volcanoes that explode along the flesh.

NCR troopers file in behind her. Form a defensive line.

A defensive line against. . .This weird, bloated sack that hangs at the center of the room. Looks like a queen ant's egg sac writ large. But pale. Pink. Throbbing.

The front of it unfurls. Leaks yellow.

The Devil's face appears. Then his arms. His chained torso.

He looks down on the NCR troopers with a sick, smug smile. Spreads his hands. The rotten things attached by thin strings of slime. "What do *you* want, kitten?"

"Uh—" Athena arches her eyebrows. "Be great to kill the shit outta you."

"You can't kill me."

Bombs and rockets shake the foundations of the bunker. Make the Devil's chains rattle.

Athena puffs her cheeks. "I mean, I know we haven't even gotten *close* to digging up the secrets of Area 51 but. . . ." She puts a hand on her hips. "You get access to Frankie's data and you turn yourself into fat sack of garbage?"

The Devil laughs. "I. . .am a *biomass*. Nothing like me has ever existed before. I can absorb *life*. I can devour the *world*."

"You're a shaved ballbag hanging on cable ties in a decrepit bunker."

"I can—"

Athena shakes her head. Unloads a full drum into the Devil's protruding face and body.

Oliver and his NCR troopers follow suit.

Bullets ruin the flesh. The fat sack that hangs with the skeleton of the Devil. Clear skin becomes a ragged bag that leaks red chunks. Then soon those chunks fall.

A rain of blood.

A rain of gore.

Athena looks to the NCR troopers.

Says, "Here is yet another asshole who makes a lotta noise then dies like a raggedy fucksuck." She sniffs. "Ain't no bite in that bark. Just a pissed off white dude thought he could make good on some other pissed off white dude's shit." She looks at the bloated, dead husk of the Devil. "At least Frankie made that shit on his own. . . ."

18.

Athena steps off Oliver's plane.

The generals are there waiting.

Dogmeat leaps away from their heels when Athena touches the tarmac. She grabs the canine by the collar. Scratches his side. Lets him lean on her.

She barks. "Okay. I did all your stupid shit. I want into the redwoods." She snaps her fingers. "Now now. Chop chop."

A male general steps forward. "You did. But your deal with Sergeant Major Bradley was to get you to *California*. Which he has done. A couple of times, in fact."

Athena bites her lip. So hard she draws blood. "I need to get to the redwoods."

The generals look to one another. A woman steps forward. "That would be New Eden. And New Eden is limited to *healthy* people and their *children*."

Athena wants to protest this but knows she's the opposite of healthy. "What can I do? What do I need to do?" She balls her fists at her sides. "The only thing I want. . .The only thing I've ever wanted is to die among the redwoods."

The NCR generals trade stares.

Oliver makes his way down the ramp. Using a rag to clean the blood from his hands. "She's worthy."

A general looks to him and says, "You'd back this woman?"

"I back her." Oliver hits the tarmac. "I say she's got more good in her than she wants. . .which might explain why she's such an asshole."

Athena arches her eyebrows.

The generals consult amongst themselves.

One of the men peels away from the pack. Looks to Athena. "We were interested in you because your leg contains technology from Frankie." He dips his head. "But it seems like your dog does as well."

Athena steps in front of Dogmeat. Puts herself between the NCR headshed and her canine. "So what."

"We would be willing to make an exception to the rules of New Eden."

". . .If."

"If you give us something useful." Pause. "Let's say the dog or your leg. Something *operational* as opposed to the mess we made at Area 51. Our key problem right now is that the Devil started eradicating his server and hard drives once our attack began. So. . .help us solve that problem."

Athena shakes her head. "You all fuckin suck."

19.

Athena tucks the crutches up into her armpits. These stupid goddamn wooden things that ain't even close to being as good as legs.

Dogmeat circles her. Follows her.

Athena says, "Yeah yeah."

She stops at the foot of a redwood in the morning light. Hasn't been that long since her surgery. She smiles. Reaches her fingers out and touches its bark. She hops on one foot so she can get close to it. Lean against its bark and smile.

Athena presses her cheek against the redwood. Smells it. Takes huge deep breaths in the hope that the smell never leaves her nostrils.

Then she picks up her crutches again.

Hobbles along the path.

Down to one of the little outposts that're supposed to house and comfort the mothers. A squat grey thing very much like a bunker.

Athena sees a hand waving.

Michelle's.

The brunette eggs her on. Eggs her farther down the path.

Athena works her way through the underbrush. The ferns. Stops next to Michelle. Sits in one of the many open seats near the woman. Wooden benches from the park that used to exist here.

Michelle's baby is gorgeous. A lumpy little thing that smiles forever. Coos. She has her mother's eyes. Thick dark hair like her uncle.

Dogmeat shoves his nose in the baby's face. Licks the new human. Which produces a giggle and then a look of total confusion on its pudgy little face.

If only Mark was around to see all of this.

Michelle lifts the baby up for Athena to hold, but the driver can't.

She has someplace to be.

Athena follows the path out. Far beyond the little safe zone for the healthy folks in the redwoods. Which is easy enough for Dogmeat to accomplish but a very literal headache for Athena and her crutches.

She sets herself down. Grunts.

Tries to ignore the fact that her brain wants her to have a right leg physically there.

She tosses the crutches. Lights a cigarette.

Everything she ever wanted is right in front of her. Ancient redwoods thick with history. A blue sea that rattles against the rocks and sprays foam.

To her ears, it's calming.

Dogmeat curls up next to her. He makes a circle then lays his snout in her lap.

Athena pets him. Leans back against one of the tress. Roots under her ass. She smokes. Watches the water.

"We made it, David."

"We made it."

ABOUT THE AUTHOR

William Vitka is a writer and journalist with more than ten books under his belt and ten years in the news business. He believes that politicians will be the doom of us all, but at least there's whiskey. His Twitter handle is @vitka and he can be found at facebook.com/VitkaWrites.

PERMUTED PRESS

needs **you** to help

SPREAD (THE) INFECTION

FOLLOW US!

f | Facebook.com/PermutedPress
🐦 | Twitter.com/PermutedPress

REVIEW US!

Wherever you buy our book, they can be reviewed! We want to know what you like!

GET INFECTED!

Sign up for our mailing list at
PermutedPress.com

PERMUTED
PRESS

14

Peter Clines

Padlocked doors.
Strange light fixtures. Mutant
cockroaches.

There are some odd things about
Nate's new apartment. Every
room in this old brownstone has
a mystery. Mysteries that stretch
back over a hundred years.
Some of them are in plain sight.
Some are behind locked doors.
And all together these mysteries
could mean the end of Nate and
his friends.

Or the end of everything…

PERMUTED
PRESS

THE JOURNAL SERIES
by Deborah D. Moore

After a major crisis rocks the nation, all supply lines are shut down. In the remote Upper Peninsula of Michigan, the small town of Moose Creek and its residents are devastated when they lose power in the middle of a brutal winter, and must struggle alone with one calamity after another.

The Journal series takes the reader head first into the fury that only Mother Nature can dish out.

PERMUTED
PRESS

Michael Clary
THE GUARDIAN | THE REGULATORS | BROKEN

When the dead rise up and take over the city, the Government is forced to close off the borders and abandon the remaining survivors. Fortunately for them, a hero is about to be chosen...a Guardian that will rise up from the ashes to fight against the dead. The series continues with Book Four: *Scratch*.

Emily Goodwin
CONTAGIOUS | DEATHLY CONTAGIOUS

During the Second Great Depression, twenty-four-year-old Orissa Penwell is forced to drop out of college when she is no longer able to pay for classes. Down on her luck, Orissa doesn't think she can sink any lower. She couldn't be more wrong. A virus breaks out across the country, leaving those that are infected crazed, aggressive and very hungry. `

The saga continues in Book Three: *Contagious Chaos* and Book Four: *The Truth is Contagious*.

PERMUTED
PRESS

THE BREADWINNER | Stevie Kopas

The end of the world is not glamorous. In a matter of days the human race was reduced to nothing more than vicious, flesh hungry creatures. There are no heroes here. Only survivors. The trilogy continues with Book Two: *Haven* and Book Three: *All Good Things*.

THE BECOMING | Jessica Meigs

As society rapidly crumbles under the hordes of infected, three people—Ethan Bennett, a Memphis police officer; Cade Alton, his best friend and former IDF sharpshooter; and Brandt Evans, a lieutenant in the US Marines—band together against the oncoming crush of death and terror sweeping across the world. The story continues with Book Two: *Ground Zero*.

THE INFECTION WAR | Craig DiLouie

As the undead awake, a small group of survivors must accept a dangerous mission into the very heart of infection. This edition features two books: *The Infection* and *The Killing Floor*.

OBJECTS OF WRATH | Sean T. Smith

The border between good and evil has always been bloody... Is humanity doomed? After the bombs rain down, the entire world is an open wound; it is in those bleeding years that William Fox becomes a man. After The Fall, nothing is certain. *Objects of Wrath* is the first book in a saga spanning four generations.

PERMUTED
PRESS

A PREPPER'S COOKBOOK

20 Years of Cooking in the Woods

by Deborah D. Moore

In the event of a disaster, it isn't enough to have food. You also have to know what to do with it.

Deborah D. Moore, author of *The Journal* series and a passionate Prepper for over twenty years, gives you step-by-step instructions on making delicious meals from the emergency pantry.

PERMUTED
PRESS